No ~~~ Romance!

No Time For Romance!

Robert Davies Higgins

© Robert Davies Higgins, 2013

Published by RDH Books

A CIP catalogue record for this book is available from the British Library.

ISBN 978-0-9926215-0-6

Prepared and printed by:

York Publishing Services Ltd
64 Hallfield Road
Layerthorpe
York YO31 7ZQ

Tel: 01904 431213

Website: www.yps-publishing.co.uk

Chapter One

Linda Cartell sank gratefully into the welcome soft embrace of her favourite armchair, kicked her shoes off, and wriggled her toes with a sigh of contentment. She was exhausted after a long day at the office, and glad, very glad indeed to be home at last.

The current recession was making the going tough, and crisis after crisis seemed to be the daily diet over the past few months, and she was beginning to feel the strain.

The telephone rang and Linda groaned as she reluctantly rose from her chair to answer it. She just reached the receiver when the answering machine took over. "Damn" she muttered, not sure whether she was annoyed with herself for not remembering to switch the machine off when she came home, or for simply forgetting that it was on in the first place, and so could have remained seated in her all too comfortable chair!

"Right my girl, something to eat, and then off to bed with you. You are definitely over-tired" she said aloud, and then shook her head and smiled, feeling rather silly as she realised that she was actually talking to herself!

A frozen chicken dinner heated in the micro provided her meagre sustenance, and then a nice warm bubble bath helped her to relax a little. There was no doubt about it, she mused, she certainly could not take many more days like this one had been!

That morning she had attended an emergency meeting of the board, when the decision was taken to close no fewer than thirty sales offices countrywide, a devastating blow.

The directors had been putting off the inevitable as long as possible, but now it was all to obvious, the Real Estate market was not merely experiencing a seasonal downturn in sales, but something more akin to a catastrophe!

The unheard of had happened, and indeed was still happening. House prices in London and the South East were actually falling! No one but no one had ever envisaged such a thing, not even in their worst nightmare!

Linda, as Personnel Director, was charged with the onerous task of notifying no fewer than six hundred and twenty four people that their services were no longer required, some of whom had given twenty plus years of their lives to the company.

Marjory, her private secretary, had sat silently as Linda dictated the redundancy letters.

"So much for loyalty, I wonder who will be the next to be fired?" Marjory said very quietly. Linda inwardly cringed, wishing that she could be anywhere in the world right at that moment, except her office.

She had worked very hard, putting in many long hours over many years to gain her present position, and it was the proudest moment of her life when she was appointed a full board member some two years ago. Now she wondered if indeed it was really worth the sacrifices she had made on a personal level, as the sarcasm in Marjory's voice stung her with its venom. This most terrible day of days had at last come to an end, and Linda let gave a sigh of relief.

Over the next few months, trading conditions went from bad to worse. Staff morale was extremely low. Redundancies, even in the head office, had alas, become a fact of life, and Linda could sense anxious eyes following her when ever she had an occasion to visit the lower floors. She had gotten to dread the very thought of going down there, and found herself delegating more and more from the sanctity of her office, whereas previously she would always have used the personal touch.

A vast knowledge of the Property Market, combined with her own skill in communicating with people on a personal level had served her well in the past, her expertise in being able to appoint the right person to the right job at the right time, had been recognised as her particular forte.

Seeing potential in someone, who perhaps did not even recognise their own talents, encouraging, even cajoling them to try a little harder, and so develop their potential, she had always been secretly proud of. Staff loyalty had been the envy of the profession. Now the situation could no longer be termed as loyalty, but more like mass exodus, indeed forced exodus in reality.

Linda sat in her office chair, staring at the rain trickling down the window pane, thinking sad thoughts.

"Linda, are you all right?" Marjory asked, "have you forgotten the board meeting? It begins in five minutes."

"Sorry, what was that? I was miles away".

"The board meeting, you only have five minutes. Are you sure you are o.k.?"

"Yes, thank you, I am fine, honestly. Goodness, I'd better get a move on!" Popping papers into a folder as she spoke, smiling to Marjory and holding up crossed fingers, Linda stepped into the hall, and purposefully strode to the boardroom.

The previous meeting had been a rather stormy one. The board had by a narrow majority, decided to hold talks with C.P.F. a large public company, listed in the top one hundred companies in the U.K. A takeover was in the offing, and Linda was utterly opposed to it.

She, along with two others was the only opposition to the proposition which had been put before them, and she had voiced very strong reservations about the reputation of C.P.F. being regarded in the city as the piranhas of the business world.

Sir Geoffrey Bottomley-Jones, the chairman of London Residential, strongly refuted Linda's objections and had advocated that the board approve the motion that he and Sir Colin Frith, the deputy chairman, be empowered to hold initial discussions with C.P.F. Sir Geoffrey carried the day on a majority vote.

Alan Arnold, the chairman of C.P.F. had built a huge worldwide conglomerate, and had the reputation of being the take-over king of the city. On a successful bid he was ruthless in breaking companies up, and selling the unwanted assets off to the highest bidders, all in the guise of "Better Management leading inexorably to maximised profit" and the bones of many such companies were strewn far and wide.

Linda was absolutely determined to fight every inch of the way to prevent London Residential falling in to the hands of such a ruthless mogul, but in her heart she knew deep down she was fighting a losing battle.

"Ahh, Linda, just the person I was hoping to see before the meeting, a quick word before it starts please?"

Linda turned to face Sir Geoffrey, and he invited her into his office.

"We'll be late for the meeting, Geoffrey" she said.

Not to worry, m'dear, the schedule has been retarded by thirty minutes at my request, please take a seat" he closed the office door as he spoke.

Linda suddenly felt very uncomfortable, and could not think for the life of her why.

"Firstly I would like to say that I have admired the tenacious way you have fought your corner on this issue, and you have to be congratulated".

For some reason, the hairs stood on the back of Linda's neck as she listened to her praise. "Thank you, Geoffrey, I assure you that there is, and never has been any personal animosity. I have only said and done what I have felt is in the best interests of the company. You and I have differing views on the way ahead for London Residential, it is as simple as that."

"Linda, I respect your judgement in most things, but in this I am afraid that you are misguided. You have formed an opinion based upon media hype written about a man you have never even met, and swallowed that hype, hook line and sinker. Now a fact of modern life is that business is undergoing a total restructuring programme, and those that fail to do so I am afraid just won't survive".

He paused to light a cigar, the continued: "Fact. Our borrowings are dangerously high. Fact: Our bankers are extremely uneasy with our trading performance, and have been making veiled treats regarding our viability, and I for one take such threats very seriously. Very seriously indeed!"

"We all do Geoffrey, but I am sure that the banks can be persuaded that our viability is not really in question" she replied as he paused to puff his enormous cigar.

"Fact," he continued, ignoring her remarks, "Alan Arnold, contrary to what you think, has a track record second to none."

Smoke billowed in great clouds as he warmed to his task, continuing, "Fact: the Arnold group of companies operate an extremely efficient cost analysis and control programme, which even the Japanese envy."

"Perhaps so, Geoffrey, but surely lack of sales is more pertinent to our problem rather than cost control, after all we have carried out swingeing cost cutting exercises recently, and I fail to see where further cuts can be found, short of closing up shop entirely" Linda said passionately.

"There is more than a hint of logic in your argument, Linda, if, and I stress IF we were to go it alone, we have precious few options open to allow us any appreciable savings. Now, this is where tying up with the Arnold Group can be of enormous benefit. Apply logic, and it is the only real solution, old girl."

"I am not convinced. If Alan Arnold can make savings beyond any we have already made, without dissecting the company and selling off the assets piecemeal, then he really is a genius. Financial backing is not the only answer, we have sufficient assets to ride the storm, and we all know this recession cannot last for ever." She retorted.

"Have you heard of British Commercial?"

"Who hasn't? They are the largest commercial and probably industrial developers in the country. Why?"

"Do you know who owns them?"

"Im not really sure" Linda replied, "but I do know that they are not owned by C.P.F"

"Quite correct. Would it surprise you to know that British Commercial is wholly owned and operated as a private company by Alan Arnold? Like ourselves, B.C. never went public, and they quietly sold to Alan Arnold some five years or so ago" he took a generous puff on his cigar, smiling at Linda with his face, but his eyes remained steely hard.

"I am astounded! How on earth could a take-over of that magnitude be made without the press finding out?"

"I told you Alan Arnold is very astute, Linda, and you should never believe all that you read in the newspapers."

"Taking control of a major company such as British Commercial is a minor miracle itself, I have to admit, Geoffrey, I also grant you that to the best of my knowledge the company is still intact, I honestly cannot recall any sell off of their assets recently" Linda conceded.

"You have hit the nail on the head, at last you are thinking with your brain m'dear. Fact is that that particular company has expanded during Alan Arnold's tenure."

"You are quite possibly correct, Geoffrey, but what I do not quite understand is what all this has to do with the proposed take-over of our company by C.P.F.?"

"That m'dear, is the crux of the matter. There is not in actual fact a bid by C.P.F. A rather unfortunate mix up on my part I'm afraid. A perfectly understandable case of putting the cart before the horse. You see, I received a phone call from Bret Gray, with a view to feel the waters on possible merger of our companies. I, on knowing that he is vice chairman of C.P.F. naturally assumed he was speaking on their behest. Unfortunately I had forgotten that he is also on the board of British Commercial" Sir Geoffrey said in his blustering fashion.

"You mean to say that we have been at loggerheads over a non existent bid? That is, to quote the vernacular, unreal, completely unreal!"

"I am sorry my dear, a slight faux pas, but, the fact that a bid is on the table is a fact nevertheless." Sir Geoffrey countered.

"Faux pas or not, Alan Arnold is still the person trying to buy our company, and no matter your arguments I doubt very much if I for one can be persuaded to change my mind." Linda replied.

"Perhaps so, but please hear me out. British Commercial put forward a proposal a few days ago, which makes a lot of sense for both companies." He took a long puff on is cigar looking intently at Linda.

"Well, Geoffrey, I'll listen to this proposal at the board meeting, but I still cannot imagine any proposal coming from Alan Arnold that won't in the long term spell disaster for this company, and may I remind you that the boardroom is the proper place to discuss such matters? She replied rather haughtily.

"You really are exasperating, Linda. I have extended you the courtesy of having a quiet word in your ear before the meeting, and I am certainly not standing for impertinence nor any emotional outburst, this is a most serious matter, and you would do well to remember that!" Sir Geoffrey fumed irately.

Linda pursed her lips, smarting at the onslaught, but she did apologise for her indiscretion.

"The plan is to merge the two companies completely, with the new designation of British Residential and Commercial. This would be a total merger Sales and administration. The savings in sales costs alone are major. We are both at present on most major high streets in the country operating and maintaining sales offices, merging them provides substantial benefits in saved rents and needless to say personnel cutbacks of course would be inevitable, but entirely necessary." He took a long slow pull on his cigar, and then continued before Linda could reply.

"Similar savings can be realised at the administration level too. We duplicate each other in almost every aspect. Locating the newly formed head office at the present site occupied by British Commercial, being the larger is the logical choice. This site would then be free for redevelopment at some later date. You know it makes perfect sense. Indeed, the perfect solution." He beamed at her, taking another contented puff of smoke.

Linda took a deep breath, wishing fervently at that moment that she had not stopped smoking. She positively trembled with anger as she studied the man standing opposite. Chairman of the board, and he was about to sell the company down the river!

"Just how many of our staff would retain their positions if this merger goes ahead?" Linda queried.

"Unfortunately some staff will have to go, but after the dust has settled, it will all be for the best."

"You are evading the question, Geoffrey. We employ over four hundred personnel here at head office. Just how may do you envisage still being in our employ after the rationalization, and how many sales personnel we currently employ will still be with us?"

"As I have said, the companies over lap in many areas, therefore it is an inevitable though albeit sad fact that there will be redundancies."

"You must have some figure in mind, Geoffrey." Linda reported.

"I can assure you that all key personnel will be retained" he replied.

Linda's dark brown eyes flashed with anger. "You are deliberately avoiding giving me a straight answer to a straight question. Surely that is not beyond you?" she positively raged.

"Ms Cartell. I shall put your raised voice down to the heat of argument, but let me assure you that everyone has to make sacrifices in time of crisis, and we must stand shoulder to shoulder and bear our share of what is a very heavy burden" Sir Geoffrey replied in a steely voice.

Linda, now furious, glared at Sir Geoffrey and said "I still wish to know just how many staff from inside this building alone do you envisage retaining their posts." Her voice was becoming shrill with emotion, and she deliberately dug her fingernails into her palms in an effort to control herself.

"As I have said, all key personnel will be retained, probably in the neighbourhood of about forty or so, give or take." He replied in a clear distinct voice.

"I beg your pardon, I couldn't have heard you correctly, and you surely did not say about forty?" she whispered.

"You heard correctly. Our best estimates forecast that number of key positions. To reiterate, we all must make sacrifices."

Linda gasped in disbelief. The others on the board would never agree to such a dastardly scheme. Saying no to Sir Geoffrey she was utterly shocked by his reply.

"I don't believe it! They simply cannot have agreed to participate in the wholesale destruction of this company!" she said, totally abhorred.

Sir Geoffrey stood to his full imposing height of six foot four and said sombrely "Everyone is agreed, Linda. It really is the only sensible step to take. I am afraid that if you do not, or cannot agree to the proposal then I shall have to insist on your resignation."

"Then you have my resignation, Sir Geoffrey" she replied solemnly.

"That is very unfortunate, I am sorry to lose you, Linda. But as I have said, we all have to make sacrifices."

Chapter Two

"I always knew that making your career number the one priority in life was a mistake, my girl. How many times have I said that you should be concentrating on finding a husband?"

"Really, Mum. I did not come over for you to lecture me over my love life. I suppose it would be too much to look for some sympathy? After all, I have given twenty odd years to the company." Linda retorted feeling rather embittered at that particular moment in time.

"Business is no place for a woman, I've always said that, and I always will. Don't come looking for sympathy from me, Linda. Sir Geoffrey what-ever his name has just done you a great service, as far as I am concerned. Now perhaps you can take some advice from your mother. Believe me, for a woman, there are more are more important things in life than a career, mark my words." Her mother said in the sagely way that mothers deem to be their right, keeping the offspring in no doubts as to who has the experience and naturally the wisdom.

"I give up, mum. You never have understood why I chose a career over a kitchen and sink."

"Please don't be upset, my dear. Of course I am sorry that things have not worked out for you the way you had hoped, but you know me, I always have been one for speaking my mind. You are not getting any younger my dear, and a good man is hard to find at any age. I just hope that you have not let your chances slip past."

"That is such an old fashioned view! Haven't you ever heard of the Emancipated Woman? I have been telling you all of my life that women have as much right as men to be in 'The Business World' as you put it, and there is a lot more to life than just marriage!" she retorted.

"And another thing, I'll have you know that I am certainly not past it!"

"I did not say that you were past it, I only said that you are getting on a bit, after all, you are in your forties, or had you forgotten that fact."

"No, Mum, I am never likely to forget it as long as you are here to remind me. How on earth did the subject of my age get into the conversation, I thought we were discussing my career?"

"I was simply pointing out that finding a husband at your age is not easy." Her mum replied coyly.

"Mum! I am not looking for a husband, not even a live in lover! And before you say anything, not even a toy boy!" Suddenly, both of them started laughing at the absurdity of their argument.

"Of course dear and I have been listening, you know. Have a nice chocolate biscuit with your tea. Try the plain one, I know that you will like it."

"Oh mum, I do wish you would stop treating me like a child, just for once. I really would like your advice on which course of action you think I should take. Please, not on the topic of some mythical husband for me?" Linda asked.

"I promise my dear, but if you would only listen to what I have been saying, and start giving it some serious thought to Linda Cartell the woman, and not just Linda Cartell the would-be tycoon, and you may find that life has far more to offer than a large office and the prestige that you have always given such credence to. Don't forget the tremendous pressure that your position placed on your shoulders, my dear, and think very seriously if it was worth it, or indeed worth doing again? That is the central question you must ask yourself, and only you know the answer to." Mrs Cartell paused to have a sip of tea.

"Now, what you need is a break away from London. Someplace nice and quiet, with no time limits, to give yourself a chance to really assess your life, and which direction you would like it to go."

"That's funny. I was just at the travel agency this morning, and picked up a few brochures. I was thinking of perhaps a week r so in Portugal."

"You haven't actually booked a holiday, have you?"

"No, I am only considering it at the moment"

"Good. I am glad. A week or so is far too a short time. You need a break, an extended break providing a complete change from your present environment." She crossed the room to the writing bureau as she spoke.

"Do you remember the holiday that your dad and I went about three years ago?"

"Of course I do. Scotland. A Highland tour"

"Yes, it was Scotland" her mum replied wistfully. "As you know, Dad and I toured the highlands for an extended three month holiday. The best of holiday we ever had."

"Care for another cup of tea, Mum? Linda asked.

"Yes please, dear. Now where was I? Oh yes. When we were in Wester Ross, we spotted a beautiful old cottage that we both fell in love with. Purple Heather Estate owned it, and somehow your Dad managed to persuade them to sell us our dream cottage. I'll never know how he managed it because it wasn't even for sale."

"You have never told me that!" Linda said in amazement.

"You were rather absorbed in you career at the time, if you remember you had just been appointed to the board, and Dad and I decided to wait until we had renovated the cottage, and then we planned to invite you to a surprise unveiling. Unfortunately, poor Henry never had the pleasure of seeing his completed wok" Mrs Cartell's eyes filled, but she bravely fought back the tears.

"Oh Mum, I am so sorry! Poor Dad, and poor you!"

Linda hugged her mother in a warm embrace. "I do love you, you know, Mum" she said tearfully.

"Anyhow, here are the keys to 'Heather Cottage'Linda. I want you to take them and go to Scotland. Not just for a few days or weeks, but for at least three months. Now I want you to promise me this."

"Three months! I cannot possibly stay away for three months, Mum! Please be reasonable." Her daughter protested.

"Of course you can, and you jolly well shall too. You need a rest. A long rest, completely removed from London. No arguing."

"I'll promise to stay for a month, Mum, but definitely no longer than that." Linda said firmly.

"That is more that I ever thought you would agree to. A deal." Came the swift reply. "Mind you, once you have experienced the tranquil beauty of the Scottish Highlands, and feel (yes I said feel) the sheer presence of the mountains, the wonderful azure of the sky on a clear day, the sparkle of the ocean and the allure of the distant islands, I am sure you shall find it as hard to leave as I did" her mum said with passion, smiling at her daughter.

"You were always a romantic at heart, Mum, you should consider getting a job with the Scottish Tourist Board" she said teasingly." You should know by now that it is the beauty of the city that stirs my blood, not the call of the wild. But I concede that in as far as me needing a rest and change of environment for a while, you are correct, and I'll go, I need to think and perhaps a cottage in the middle of nowhere is just what I require right now. Thank you, Mum, I truly wish that it were you and Dad going instead of me" she concluded giving her Mum a great big hug.

"I know, dear, and thank you, but you know that your Dad would be really happy to know that his own very special cottage was now proving to be of importance and hopefully, of some benefit to his daughter, who was always the apple of his eye" Mrs Cartell pressed the keys into Linda's hand.

"Why don't you come with me, Mum? Please. I would really enjoy having your company, and it is a long time since we went anywhere together" Linda leaded.

"We'll go some other time. I want you to go and enjoy a really good rest, forget abut business and try and learn to relax. I am positive you have forgotten how to, and I would only be a distraction. You'd never be done fussing over me, so, no, you must go alone."

"You win," Linda submitted, "but if you should change your mind, phone me tonight. I promise that I'll leave first thing in the morning."

"I am glad to hear it, by the way, speaking of phones, we had one installed in the cottage. I have been meaning to have it disconnected every time the account for the standing charges arrives, and then of course, you know my memory, I forget again."

"Trust you, Mum. But I am sure that I won't complain about your forgetfulness once I am installed in the wilderness." Linda said teasingly.

"I am a firm believer that there is a reason for everything, and my poor memory has proved to be a blessing in disguise, at least you'll have the safety net of having the means to contact "civilisation" should you become desperate." Her Mum quipped.

"You are incorrigible, Mum" Linda replied with her tongue in cheek.

That evening Linda packed her cases, and the studied the map of Great Britain, She had never been to Scotland, and didn't really know what to expect. She was a city dweller through and through, and had never harboured the slightest notion to visit the countryside let alone the wilds of Northern Scotland, and the very thought filled her with trepidation.

The scant knowledge, she had of the highlands came for the odd TV programme, and as far as she could recall the place was populated with an indigenous dour people who held all the English in a very low esteem, all entirely based on something to do with Bonnie Prince Charlie, about two hundred years ago!

She lit a welcomed cigarette (she has started smoking again), poured a coffee, and hoped fervently that she had not made the most terrible mistake, but consoled herself with the knowledge that one could not always believe what one was told was fact as being necessarily so, especially when the source of information was a television documentary!

"I suppose that a month is not exactly a life sentence" she said to her reflection in the dressing table mirror as she prepared for bed. Mum would never change she mused, it seemed to Linda that Mary Cantrell's sole aim in life was to see her only child married off, a singular desire to achieve (Linda's) 'happiness', whether she wanted it or not!

The brush swept easily through her auburn hair, making he feel relaxed. The light reflected off her curls, showing a deep even copper, her own natural colour, with not a grey hair in sight. A few faint lines around the eyes, and dark and sultry, she had once been told by a former boyfriend, sending her into fits of laughter at the time, much to her would be lover's chagrin! Smiling at the memory, she exposed a row of brilliant white teeth.

"Not too bad for forty six, girl, but then again, you are no spring chicken either" she commented to her image smiling at her from the mirror.

Glancing at the full length mirrors on the wardrobe doors as she stood up, she paused to look at her reflection. Tall and slim, with a 36-26-36 figure, with a firm bust line did not present too bad an impression she supposed, but the very idea that she would someday meet her prince charming, as her mother fervently hoped, was an utterly ludicrous notion. At forty six no less, how absurd!

She knew only too well that men regarded middle aged women as easy prey for a short fling, certainly not as serious relationship prospects!

Romance had seemed important once upon a time, a long time ago now, she reflected, but having been let down very badly by the man she had loved very deeply, Linda had sworn to herself that she would never place any man before herself or her career ever again.

This was a conscious decision made out of heartache, but a decision that se had adhered to since, and had never regretted. Naturally there were times when she had been lonely, and the comfort of a man's loving arms around her would have been most welcome, but the loneliness would always dissipate with time, and of course she had always had her work to occupy her mind. Mum may just be right, she thought on reflection, with no career to fall back on for a crutch in the immediate future, she really did have a lot of thinking to do, and decisions to make.

Moving closer to the mirror she looked deeply into her dark brown eyes. Life could never be the same again; she knew this to be certain now. Would loneliness come to be her unwelcome companion? A cold shiver ran down her spine, and she gave an involuntary shudder. For the first time in many years, Linda Cartell was feeling more than a little unsure of herself.

"Right my girl, pull your self together! Get to bed. A good night's rest, and then it is off to Scotland with you in the morning, and no more silly fears!" She scolded her reflection, got into bed and put out the light and closed her eyes, but sleep proved to be very elusive and very fitful when eventually it did come.

Chapter Three

The melodic sounds of Mike Oldfield's 'Tubular bells' enveloped the interior of the Jaguar as it sped northwards. Linda was lost in the music, and time and distance slipped past effortlessly. The cassette ended, and Linda breathed a little sigh of contentment. Glancing at the dashboard clock, she was very surprised to see that it was gone two thirty p.m.

She had departed at eight that morning, and the journey through town was a nightmare as per usual any morning in London, offering the erstwhile traveller frustration and boredom as their bill of fare. Gaining the motorway at last, much to her horror the traffic was at its best never quicker than a crawl, more often than not at a standstill, all the way to Birmingham, due to endless road works!

Once north of the Greater Birmingham conurbation, the ceaseless traffic cones ended at last, and as if by magic, the traffic suddenly was moving at the speed limit! She was fairly on edge by then, after what had seemed an eternity to her of stop start driving, and gratefully she pulled into the first service area on the M6 to enjoy a very refreshing cup of coffee and a sandwich.

Relaxed after a far longer than intended break, Linda had set off at once, and for the first time since leaving the house actually began to enjoy the freedom that driving can offer, and appreciate the luxury which the Jaguar is famed for. The car was part of the settlement she had agreed with the company on her departure, and until now had regarded the vehicle as a prestige symbol. Now for the first time she was experiencing the thrill of driving this fabulous machine out on the open road. The slightest touch on the accelerator was almost frightening to her, the acceleration was simply electrifying, and the sensation of speed gave her a sense of freedom which was awesome!

Crossing the border into Scotland filled her briefly with trepidation, but she soon relaxed once more as she became once again engrossed in her driving. The sound of her favourite music gently caressing her senses soon overcame her active mind, and she became oblivious to where she was or what she was even doing there!

Large hills swept past as the powerful car sped on up the M74, and she was vaguely aware of black faced sheep grazing on the slopes, and she marvelled at how they managed to cling on to such steep sides, unconcernedly munching at the grass. Suddenly the hills seemed to have evaporated, and civilisation once more engulfed her as she approached the outskirts of Glasgow.

The traffic became heavier, but nothing compared to London, she thought, but never the less, she soon found that she had to give the road her full attention as she approached the city centre, and was quite annoyed to find that her reverie was all too soon evaporated as once again she experienced stop and start driving that day!

Once clear of Glasgow, which was far larger than she had expected, the traffic flow gained its equilibrium with the intended speed limit, and Linda began to enjoy herself again, the tribulations of the slow progress through the city soon forgotten as she once more revelled in the sheer delights of the Jaguar.

A sign stating motorway services five miles caught her attention, and she suddenly became aware that she was actually hungry. A few minutes later the Jaguar pulled into the parking lot of one of the larger restaurant chains which vie for business along Britain's motorways

The large self-service facility had an adequate menu on offer, and Linda eventually settled for a sirloin steak with all the trimmings, and yielded to the temptation of a scrumptious apple turnover laced with fresh whipped cream!

She thoroughly enjoyed the meal, although an occasional twinge of guilt had gnawed at her as she succumbed to the intrinsic delights of the dessert. She banished the thought of the undoubtedly catastrophic calorie count of the light puff pastry and fresh cream to the back of her mind, with the justification that she was after all on holiday, and most definitely deserved a little self pampering.

Passing the gift shop in the foyer, Linda spotted those extra long cigarettes that are rolled in liquorice paper, and bought a pack on impulse. Her mind was still in turmoil, and somehow this long brown cigarette took on the significance of a public show of defiance to all male chauvinists of this world that she, Linda Cartell, could and would do exactly as she pleased, and had the freedom to do so without the handicap of a man to tell her otherwise!

The memory of where she was actually going to for the next month suddenly struck her, and she turned and re-entered the shop and purchased another six hundred of the cigarettes. At least she may have promised her mother that she would spend an entire four weeks in the middle of nowhere, but at least she would have some vestiges of civilisation with her, she determined!

"Excuse me, ma'am, do you know the name of the castle over there?" a voice in a strong Texan accent asked.

"M'mm, what was that….I am sorry, I was miles away, Linda apologised.

"That's all right ma'am, I was just asking if you knew the name of the castle?" he repeated.

"Oh. I see." Linda followed the direction in which the man was pointing. A large medieval fortress perched on the top of an imposing hill, dominating the surrounding valley (or would that be a glen? She wondered) affording the castle a commanding view in every direction and what must have been an almost impenetrable defensive position in the days of the bow and arrow.

"Well, I am a stranger myself, but I know that the town behind the castle is called Stirling, so I think that the castle bears the same name, if memory serves me correctly from my school history. I am sorry I cannot be more of a help."

"Nothing to apologise for, ma'am, I reckon it probably is Stirling castle, what do you reckon honey?" he asked his wife.

"I told you when I was looking at the map that it was Stirling castle, but you never reckon that I can think for myself, Gus. And you know what, darling?" she said to Linda, "If we all knew as much as he does, then we'd still know nothing!, Smiling she returned to the restaurant in triumph.

"Excuse the little lady, ma'am," the flustered Texan said, "thanks again for your help, and have a nice day now. You hear?" and rather sheepishly he too returned to the relative safety of the restaurant.

Feeling slightly embarrassed, Linda made for the sanctity of her car, but Stirling and its castle seemed to draw her like a magnet. She had intended driving straight through to Heather Cottage when she left London, but the lure of the castle proved to be too strong, and she decided to check into the motel which was adjacent to the restaurant instead.

After a nice hot shower and a change of clothing, she went to the reception to pick up some brochures on Stirling and the castle.

"Have you never been to Stirling before?" the receptionist asked her in a soft Scottish accent.

"No, in fact this is my first time in Scotland, I am afraid I have to admit" she replied.

"Well I am sure you will love it here, and I just know that you will love Stirling. Apart from the castle of course, and the obligatory tourist gift shops, the city boasts an excellent variety of fashion outlets. The usual large chain stores found in most British high streets, but we have some really exquisite boutiques as well, comparable to anything that London has to offer" the receptionist said.

"Wow! That is some claim! Are you sure that you don't work for the tourist board?" Linda asked jokingly.

"No. I am just proud of my hometown, I suppose. But wait till you see the prices compared to London, I'm sure that you will agree with me. Honestly!" she stressed with the utmost conviction.

"You have convinced me; I'll go and have a look at your town that you are so proud of." Linda replied with a smile.

"You won't be sorry, I promise. I lived in London for a time, dazzled by the lure of the bright lights, I guess. I used to think of Stirling as the parochial back water. Living in London taught me a lot, in particular that the grass is not always greener on the other side." The girl answered truthfully.

"Thank you for your advice, but I still think that London is probably more my style, more sophisticated, perhaps? Linda commented.

"No offence intended, madam, I assure you" the receptionist said hurriedly." I didn't mean to cast aspersions on London, it was an experience that I would not have wanted to have missed, but it can be a lonely place, despite its size, and I was probably a wee bit homesick as well"

"I assure you that I will not take offence at anything you have said, as a matter of fact I have thoroughly enjoyed our conversation, and you have been very informative. I know that London can be a very lonely place for some people. Being a Londoner born and bred, it's something I have never experienced. But, on the other hand, being a Londoner I can envisage a person feeling very lonely living away up here!" she said with a laugh. "You know I think I'll follow your advice and see what your home town has to offer" she smiled sweetly to the receptionist and made her way to the Jaguar.

Later that evening Linda stood admiring herself in front of the mirror in the hotel bedroom. There was no doubt about it, she thought, the girl in reception really knew her home town!

Thanks to her guidance, Linda had just spent one of the most enjoyable afternoons that she had had in many a long day. The shopping was wonderful, and she, Linda Cartell, London sophisticate, who had shopped in the best Boutiques that London, Paris, Rome and New York had to offer a girl, had been totally amazed by the variety, quality and style that the fashion boutiques of Stirling had to offer!

Three suits, two dresses, and no fewer than five tops and three pairs of jeans attested not only to the quality, but as her mentor had promised, amazingly low prices compared to London! Scotland was suddenly not looking such a bad prospect after all, she mused.

She felt a twinge of guilt as she folded her purchases and neatly packed them into the new suitcase she had bought at the last minute before she finally left Stirling and headed back to the motel. She had never intended to buy anything, but when confronted by the array of style and quality which had frankly astounded her, and then the prices compared to London. She simply could not resist, and had gone more than a little overboard!

Happily, she justified her spending spree to herself with the knowledge that she was on holiday, after all, wasn't spending money and indulging oneself part of the holiday experience? That night she slept soundly, and woke refreshed, ready for anything that the world had to put her way.

Before departing, she sought out Gillian the receptionist who had been so helpful, and gave her a small gift she had purchased for her in Stirling. The gold chain and pendant was more than an adequate thank you, and young Gillian McBain was over the moon! Linda was only too pleased to have given the girl some small pleasure in return for the absolute sheer joy and release that she had experienced indulging herself with such carefree abandon in the boutiques after the tremendous strain that she had been under for such a long time. Gillian McBain had no idea what a help she had been, an angel in disguise, and blissfully unaware of it, thought Linda.

The sun shone brightly as the sleek Jaguar pulled onto the motorway. She sat perfectly relaxed behind the wheel, humming along to the James Last orchestra's rendition of the Beatles 'Norwegian Wood'.

The rolling green hills and rich farming countryside surrounding her provided the perfect backdrop to the music, and the miles disappeared almost imperceptibly.

Perth, known as the 'Gateway to the Highlands' was gained in no time. As she approached the large traffic roundabout on the outskirts of the city, she hesitated momentarily as the thought of taking a side trip into the city tempted for a fleeting moment, but she smiled to herself and made a left turn onto the A9 and headed for Inverness. Self indulgence could be taken too far, she reflected!

The trip was proving to be far better than she had dared to hope, encountering no major roadwork's at all, much to her relief. She made a brief stop for lunch at Inverness, and then followed the route around the top of the famous Loch Ness to the village of Drummnadrochit, which boasts the Loch Ness Monster centre as its main claim to fame.

The views of the loch which the road afforded the driver were few and far between, Linda thought, but when she did manage to catch a glimpse, the water had not as much as a ripple disturbing the surface, let alone afford a rare view of the monster to this city girl! She had been secretly hoping that 'Nessie' would put in an appearance for her benefit, but Goodness only knows what she would have done if it had obliged!

Giving the loch a last glance, she turned right onto the A887 at Invermoriston, and headed for Kyle of Loch Alsh. She admitted to having experienced a certain thrill at having seen Loch Ness for herself. She had, of course always dismissed the stories of the existence of such a thing as a monster in the loch as stuff and nonsense, but having seen and felt the magic of Loch Ness that many people testify to having experienced, who was she to dispute those who claimed to have indeed seen a monster?

The scenery grew ever more spectacular with each passing mile, and music filled the air as Linda increased the volume on the car stereo, as the beauty and sheer majesty of the mountains completely enraptured her. Feeling a sense of happiness that she had never before experienced, and of being aware of feeling so vitally alive! What an utterly wonderful feeling, she thought.

All too soon she reached the village of Achnasheen, where she stopped at the railway station coffee shop to use the restroom and have a welcome break and a cup of coffee. Staring at the mountains surrounding her as she sipped the warm liquid, her mind drifted back to her short shopping spree in Stirling the day before and thought how the topography had changed in such a short distance.

Stirling was protected by gentle rolling hills, and now a few hours away she was in the midst of truly spectacular mountains. She suddenly stopped her movement halfway to taking another sip of coffee as though thunderstruck. Stirling. She had completely forgotten to visit the castle! She had been so absorbed in the shops that what she had initially intended to see she had utterly forgotten about! She resolved then and there to visit the castle on the return journey. How could she have been so remiss, she wondered?

Opening her handbag she took out the map her mother had given her, and, yes, she had remembered correctly, this was where she took the left hand fork in the road and headed west to Loch Duich, the road famed in the song the 'Road to the Isles.'

Linda enjoyed the road immensely, the weather and scenery both being superb. "Good old Mum" she said aloud, "I am so glad that you insisted that I come, although I probably would never actually admit it to you in person". She added, smiling widely.

Chapter Four

Reaching Loch Duich, Linda slowed the car down to make certain that she did not miss the turn coming up on the right. Her mother had stressed the point that it was an exceedingly narrow single track road the like of which Linda had no experience of, and apart from driving along it very carefully, she also had to take care that she did not drive past it in the first place!

She spotted the junction ahead and engaged the right hand turning signal, the Jaguar slowed to almost a crawl as she engaged second gear to manoeuvre the tight turn. Suddenly the car seemed to acquire the dimensions of a whale as she turned onto the narrow track that was jokingly designated as a B road on her map! Good God, it was no more than a track, she mused. The Jaguar's bonnet filled the entire width of it, and at that moment Linda wished fervently that she had been given a mini as a parting gift from the company instead!

For the first time since passing her driving test many years before, she was full of apprehension behind the wheel of a car. This narrow ribbon of asphalt wound and twisted and turned like a demented reptile, and seemed to go on for simply ever, even worse, it was heading straight up to the top of the mountain!

Slowly, ever so slowly, she negotiated the large vehicle ever onward and upwards, her heart in her mouth. Every so often there was what seemed to her an extremely miserly widening of the road with the sign 'PASSING PLACE ONLY' boldly stated on it. She passionately prayed that she would not encounter so much as a bicycle on this nightmare let alone a car!

After a heart-stopping eternity of never ending blind curves she at last bridged the summit of this horrendous mountain, extremely grateful that she had not had the misfortune to have met anyone coming form the opposite direction. She sighed deeply, relieved that the ordeal was over, and began the painstakingly slow, and, in her estimation, exceedingly perilous descent to the floor of the glen far below.

Immediately ahead lay a hairpin bend; Linda slowed to a snail's pace, sounded the horn, and nervously steered hard left. A low metal crash barrier ran along the right side of the road, the other side of which was a sheer drop of several hundred feet. She was, to say the least, terrified!

Her heart was pounding like a sledgehammer in her chest, as she watched in fascination as the huge bulk of the Jaguar glided smoothly round the curve. "What on earth do I do now if I meet anything coming up the way?" she said to the car, as panic began to grip with its icy fingers of doom.

Suddenly the road straightened, and slowly Linda began to calm down again. As she regained her composure she looked up and gasped at the beauty which appeared in her vision, as she descended onto the most breath taking valley she had ever seen. Wait a minute, she thought, not a valley, a GLEN, this is Scotland!

The lush green fields, with black faced sheep simply everywhere, yielded to a plantation of assiduous trees on the valley floor. The road widened perceptibly, and soon she was driving along an avenue of beech trees, their shadows enveloping the Jaguar in a velvety blanket of twilight.

An opening loomed ahead and a varnished wooden oak sign announced that one was now entering Purple Heather Estates. A driveway cut off to the right, but a few yards farther on it took a sharp left and was swallowed by the trees, obscuring the gaze of any too curious eyes. Linda knew from what her mum had described that the mansion house was at the foot of that drive, and she wondered if she would have the opportunity to see it whilst she was here.

A mile or so on, the trees ended as suddenly as they had appeared, giving way once more to fields and the ubiquitous sheep. The end of the glen was reached, and Linda inwardly groaned as the road began to climb again!

However, the road builders had been kinder this time, with no terrifying bends, and the width was kept at a reasonable standard. Her trepidation gradually subsided. The jaguar positively purred up the hillside, and she was quite relaxed as she crested the summit.

She screamed in abject terror, slammed the brakes and released her grip on the steering wheel all in one motion, the car veered to the left and the front left wheel ended in the ditch which ran alongside the road!

Six highland Cattle stood nonplussed in the centre of the road, quite unconcerned by the scene that confronted them. They had witnessed similar situations before!

Linda sat gripping the steering wheel so tightly her knuckles shone white, as one of the great hairy beasts, with the largest set of horns she had ever seen ambled up to the car, and pressed its great moist nose against her window and snorted heavily.

Poor Linda was gripped with fear as she stared at the ferocious monster, wondering what to do, and too terrified to do it even if she had known! In her fright, she failed to notice the Range Rover pull up behind.

A tall man with dark hair greying at the temples emerged form the vehicle and clapped his hands loudly. The cattle immediately took fright and scattered in all directions.

"Are you alright?" he questioned as he approached the Jaguar, a friendly (or was it amused, Linda reflected later that evening?) smile showing beneath twinkling eyes.

"Thank you!" Linda said with relief in her voice. "I was absolutely terrified! I am not hurt; I was just scared out of my wits by that ferocious bull"

"I am glad you are not injured" her knight errant replied, "but I feel that I ought to point out that the ferocious bull happens to be a cow! "Her name is Petal, and I assure you that she was only being curious, and did not mean you any harm" he was grinning widely, which unfortunately only served to raise Linda's ire.

"Curious!?" she fumed "Well, bull or cow, that animal is down right dangerous, and should certainly not be allowed to roam free! I think it is an absolute disgrace, and I intend to report this matter to the proper authorities as soon as I reach my destination."

"I do realise that you have suffered a fright, and you are naturally upset, but I assure you in all honesty that Petal and her sisters are completely docile, in fact they really are as harmless as kittens, despite their fearsome appearance."

"You surely do not seriously expect me to believe that? Any fool can see just how wild they are!" she raged.

"Please try and calm yourself. They are docile, as I have stated, and I can also assure you that the cows have every legal right to be here, madam. Didn't you notice the signs warning you to look out for loose sheep and cattle on the road? I can assure you that there are plenty of them, and it is entirely your responsibility to drive carefully and be on the lookout for animals, not the reverse!" He retorted, becoming rather irritated with the emotional female, much to his own annoyance at doing so! He rarely lost his temper, but she was now becoming a pain in the rear!

"Road signs? I don't care about road signs. Look at my car! That animal was trying to attack me!" Linda stormed. "Wait a minute; you seem to know a lot about this cow."

"Well, I am almost afraid to tell you, but I must admit, Petal and the others are indeed mine." He said with more than a little trepidation, not at all sure as to the reaction this news would have on this very attractive, but very annoyed lady!

"I should have known. No wonder you are defending them so stoutly. Well take due notice, sir, you have certainly not heard the last of this matter" Linda replied with an air of self rightousness.

"I am quite certain of that, believe me. I can only apologise for your inconvenience, and obvious scare, but I must reiterate madam that the cattle have every right to be here, and it is entirely up to the motorist to take proper care and attention, and to be alert at all times. One cannot hold the cattle responsible. I am sure you will see reason when you have had time to reflect on this." The man replied in a soft yet firm tone.

"Typical male chauvinist attitude. You obviously think that because I am a woman that what you say must be right, silly little female should be put in her place!"

"I never mentioned your gender. The fact that you are a female is completely irrelevant! You obviously have a chip on your shoulder, lady. As a matter of fact I was really thinking that you are typical of all city dwellers, arrogant, but unfortunately ignorant of country ways, and your sex has no bearing on ignorance. Ignorance does not recognise gender, only those foolish enough to embrace it!" he, now rather having second thoughts on his own wisdom at having rescued her, (much to his own astonishment) answered.

Linda suddenly felt very foolish, and felt her cheeks begin to burn with embarrassment. "I am sorry. I did say some things which I shouldn't have, and I apologise. But I got such a fright, and these great hairy beasts are very intimidating."

"We both got a little over heated, I guess." He replied gallantly, "now why don't we begin again?" he opened the car door as he spoke, and gave Linda a helping hand to exit the vehicle. "Are you quite sure that you are not hurt?"

Linda smiled and assured him that she was fine. She became aware for the first time just what a strikingly handsome man he was, with his deeply tanned skin, and vivid blue eyes, which, despite their heated exchange only a few moments before, shone with obvious good nature. They just have that certain twinkle that is so rare, she thought.

"I am glad that you really are fine; now let's take a look at your car." He walked around and bent down and examined the wheel that was in the ditch. "Well, there doesn't seem to be any damage done, you were very fortunate. I'll have to tow you out of the ditch, only take a moment" he said quite cheerfully.

"Are you sure the wing is not damaged? It seemed to make a terrible bang."

"Positive. You'll see for yourself in a minute, when she is pulled clear of the ditch." He replied cheerily, "you see the bank is mainly moss, spagnum moss, and it cushioned the blow. Just a bit of dirt on the wing, you were lucky you went off at this point." He was working as he spoke.

Having secured the tow rope, he instructed Linda to get into the Jaguar and steer when he pulled it free with the powerful Range Rover, and a moment later her car was safely back on the road.

Linda gave a huge sigh of relief, and then rushed around to inspect the wing. He was of course correct. The car was perfect except for a little dirt.

"By the way, I meant to ask you what you are doing on this road, are you lost?" He undid the tow rope as he spoke.

"Being up here in the middle of the wilds I suppose that that is a reasonable assumption to make, but no, I am not lost, actually. I am going to Heather Cottage. Have you heard of it by any chance?" Linda asked.

"Ah, then you must be Linda Cartell. We were not sure when you would be arriving." He said to her astonishment.

"How on earth do you know who I am? Don't answer that, I know. My mother!"

"That's right, she telephoned the estate office to inform us of your imminent arrival, to make sure that no one would take you for a burglar." He laughed.

"Trust Mum" Linda said, shaking her head, only she would think of that. Well, I would like to thank you for rescuing me, and I really am sorry we got off on the wrong foot, Mr... I am afraid you have me at a disadvantage"

"Oh dear, I am sorry. I do apologise. I am Alan Ferguson" he said offering his hand, now if you care to pull into the passing place just ahead, I'll go in front and take you to Heather Cottage." He smiled charmingly at her, and her heart gave a little leap.

"Thank you very kindly" she said, "but I would not want to inconvenience you any further" she protested, but secretly hoped that he would ignore her request and indeed lead the way!

"Nonsense, I am going that direction anyway to home farm, and I am sure that Mrs Campbell will be very glad to see you, she is the house keeper at the farm, and I know that she has a meal prepared for you" he explained.

"How kind. I never expected a welcome like this, in fact I never expected a welcome at all. I am flabbergasted, actually. Goodness only knows what you must think of me after my inexcusable outburst earlier, I am feeling rather ashamed of myself" she said hanging her head.

" I assure you that the incident, if you could call it such, is totally dismissed from my memory, it never happened, we, if you recall, started afresh." Alan said firmly.

"Thank you. In London no one would think of making sure that a stranger had everything that they required to start their holiday, I guess kindness and courtesy have long since been left by the wayside, regretfully." She replied sincerely.

"Think nothing of it. I am sure that you will love Heather Cottage, and, you can never tell, you might even grow to love highland cattle!"

"Now, that would take a miracle!" she said giggling at the thought.

As she followed the Range Rover along the road, she could not help thinking on what a charming and definitely handsome man Alan Ferguson was. The eyes! She had never seen such vivid blue eyes in her life, they were simply…dazzling, was the best description she could think of.

She gave a wistful sigh. Some lucky woman undoubtedly had this most masculine of men all to herself, and, probably being madly in love, he thought her wonderful too! Reflecting on her own childish performance over the past half hour, she was in no doubt as to what his opinion of her must be. A spoiled brat of a woman with the temper of a Tasmanian devil, and the intelligence of a raving lunatic!

Chapter Five

The sensation of the most beautiful white sand that Linda had ever seen, trickling between her toes was very pleasing to her as she walked barefoot along the shore of the sea loch which lay only a few hundred yards from her now beloved Heather Cottage.

The air was warming in the spring sunshine, and she had removed her shoes a few moments before, as the sand looked so tempting, she felt like a child again, but was thoroughly enjoying herself, and knew there was no one around to make her feel self conscious, it was a wonderful feeling of freedom. Her new jeans hugged her tightly, as did the polo necked sweater she had purchased in Stirling, showing her figure to great advantage, not that there was anyone to notice, but she felt good, and happy with herself and the world.

She had been at the cottage two days now, and it was all she could ever hope for. Her dad had accomplished a splendid piece of work in his design. The structure itself was over two hundred years old, and the only exterior alterations Mr Cartell had made were double glazed lattice windows and a new slated roof.

The interior was a sheer joy to Linda. The living room was panelled from floor to ceiling in V shaped polished pine wood. The ceiling was still supported by the original wooden beams, with the same design in pine wood carried through from the walls. The overall effect was stunning.

Under floor oil-fired central heating had been installed providing comfort for the occupant to combat the cool Scottish climate. The fact that there were no radiators Linda found very pleasing to the eye.

Rich Wilton carpeting cosseted the floor, and brass oil lamp style wall lighting gave the room an air of the romantic past, with the convenience of the modern.

The kitchen had all that she could wish for, with every gadget that was available to the modern cook installed. The cupboards were in rosewood with leaded glass doors. The cooker was the latest in modern design, with touch top hobs, overhead grill and oven, surmounted with a beaten copper extractor chimney.

Double stainless steel sinks, a garbage disposal unit to make life easy. Adequate work tops providing the cook with plenty of elbow room. A dishwasher, and of course a nifty microwave oven with roasting facilities completed the appliances.

A breakfast bar with custom made high stools, Linda was exceptionally pleased with. A safety swivel mounted jug kettle and coffee pot was one of the cleverest innovations she had ever seen, enabling the user to pour boiling water and coffee without having to lift either a kettle or pot, it was brilliant! The kitchen was lit with conventional fluorescent strip lighting, providing an even shadow free light overall.

Thinking of the kitchen brought a smile to Linda. When she and Alan arrived at the cottage, Mrs Campbell was there as he had forecast.

She was in the kitchen, "Brought in a few supplies to tide you over dear," she said. The home farm house keeper had stocked the cupboards with every conceivable item that Linda could have wished for. Fresh free range eggs, milk, butter and cheese were all home produced on the farm, and the bread was made by Mrs Campbell herself. "When you live in the country you soon learn to be self sufficient when Linda showed surprised to learn that anyone actually baked bread for themselves!

Quite overwhelmed at this kindness, Linda expressed her gratitude to Mrs Campbell who blushed in embarrassment.

"No more than anyone would do for a neighbour, my dear. I am sure you would have done the same for me if the shoe was on the other foot, and by the way, call me Jeannie, please. Being addressed as Mrs Campbell makes me feel ancient!" the large rosy cheeked woman smiled warmly and Linda warmed to her immediately, she was positive that they would get along famously.

The sound of the Range Rover approaching reached Linda long before she could see it. Sound carried a long way in the tranquillity of the country, and Linda was still trying to adjust to this phenomenon. She was just opening the cottage door as the vehicle appeared in the distance.

Alan smiled as he drew to a stop, and Linda felt an air of excitement as she greeted him.

"Good morning. How are you settling in, Linda?" He smiled broadly as he spoke. "Sorry I haven't been over sooner, but the pressures of business, and all that, you know."

"I know about the pressures of business all too well" she replied, "I am settling in extremely well, thank you. I simply love the cottage, and this place. You are very fortunate to live and work in such a beautiful and peaceful environment, Alan. Although I imagine running an estate must have its own problems."

"A few now and then, but nothing too earth shattering. I encounter far more problems from interests I hold out with the estate. That brings me to my main reason for being here. I have to go on a short business trip tomorrow, and I was wondering if you would care to join me? I thought perhaps you would enjoy seeing some of the local countryside. We will of course be home by evening." His deep blue eyes looked deeply into hers and she felt her knees trembling, a sensation she had not experienced since she was a school girl.

"I would love to, Alan" she replied, rather too quickly, she scolded herself trying to keep her voice steady. "I am looking forward to it already" she did hope that she was not gushing like a silly adolescent. She was also extremely annoyed and perplexed by the fact that a man should have this affect on her!

"Great! I'll pick you up around seven thirty in the morning. I hope that is not too early for you?"

"No. Seven thirty is just fine" she lied. Those eyes! One could drift forever gazing into them, she mused. Snapping back to reality, she invited him in for coffee.

"I would really a coffee with you, Linda, but I am afraid that business dictates that I must return to the office. I look forward to seeing you in the morning. Bye for now." With these parting words he was gone.

Sipping her coffee Linda suddenly realised that she had forgotten to ask where they were going! She smiled and shook her head ruefully. The awesome pull of a certain pair of dark blue eyes were definitely disconcerting!

"Are you at home, Linda?" Jeannie Campbell's voice rang out, her head popping round the door, a friendly smile beaming at Linda.

"Come in, Jeannie, you must have smelled the coffee. I have just percolated a fresh pot" Linda said, happy to see her new friend.

"Do you enjoy a bit of fish?" Jeannie asked as she entered the kitchen.

"I am very partial to fish, as it happens. As a matter of fact, it is probably my favourite food" Linda replied.

"Good. Two of the boys were out this morning, and I brought you a little of their catch. I thought you may like them for lunch" Jeannie said as she'd place two freshly caught whiting, all nicely cleaned, on the kitchen table.

"They look truly wonderful Jeannie. Thank you kindly, I am looking forward to them already." Linda said.

"I was not too sure whether to fillet them or not, so I decided to leave them whole. I'm not being impertinent, but have you ever filleted fish before?" Jeannie asked.

Linda shook her head and had to admit that filleting fish was definitely not one of the skills she had acquired in life.

"I thought that it would be unlikely" Jeannie replied. "Now you take a seat and sit down and I'll show you the correct way to fillet, and who knows? Perhaps it could stand you in stead in the future." She took a sharp knife from the rack as she spoke, and set about her task skilfully, instructing Linda all the while as she deftly skinned and boned the fish.

Linda watched in admiration as Jeannie wielded the razor sharp knife with all the skill of a surgeon, her tongue never halting for a second.

"Now, I'm not saying that a squeeze of lemon juice is not nice with a bit of whiting, but I prefer to serve it with nice pieces of pineapple, the bitter-sweet taste compliments the creamy texture of newly caught whiting to perfection. You should give it a try. My! I am making my own mouth water at the thought" Jeannie laughed heartily.

"Thank you again for the fish and the instruction, I assure you that I shall follow your cooking suggesting to the letter" Linda said sincerely. "You have just missed Alan, he left a few moments before you arrived."

"I thought I heard his car when I was cycling over here. Just in for a wee chat, was he?"

"Actually, he came to invite me to accompany him on a business trip he is making tomorrow. He very kindly gave me the offer. I really appreciate the fact he thought of me. It was very kind of him and will give me the opportunity to see the local countryside. He is an extremely nice man isn't he?" Linda said.

"Aye, he is that. One of the nicest men you could ever wish to meet" Jeannie replied.

"I am beginning to think so" said Linda. "His wife is a very fortunate woman."

"Alan lost his wife years ago, it was such a tragic event. Mary, that was his wife, Arnold his brother and his wife Alexandra with their two children, Tina and Robbie, were on their way to Kenya for a holiday. Alan was to join them a few days later. Unfortunately, their plane never arrived. It was blown out of the sky by terrorists. They were all killed. Alan was devastated, and has more or less been a recluse ever sine. Business became his sole consuming passion, and probably saved his sanity. But, that all happened fifteen years ago. It is not healthy for a man to shut himself off from life forever." Jeannie sighed a little sigh and then said "You must have something special my dear, you are the first woman he has actually shown an interest in, all those years, I mean even to talk to" Jeannie smiled sweetly at Linda.

"That is terribly, terribly sad. What an awful tragedy for anyone to endure. Poor Alan! I knew nothing of this, Jeannie, and I am very grateful to you for telling me, I really don't know what else to say. It is beyond words." Linda said, sadness and disbelief in her voice.

"Aye, well, it was a long time ago now, and it's not before time that Alan started to live again. Sad as it may be, life must go on, or what is the point? Now don't you go feeling guilty when you are around him. The past is the past, and you my lass are in the present. Remember that" Jeannie advised. They sat in silence for a while, each lost in their thoughts.

"Where are you going tomorrow?" Jeannie asked.

"You know. Alan came in and out so quickly, I forgot to ask, Linda replied rather sheepishly.

"A wee bit distracted by those dark blue eyes, I'll bet!" Jeannie said teasingly.

"I was not!" Linda protested, nervously lighting a cigarette. "Alan is obviously one of nature's gentlemen, a rarity in this world, and he is just extending the hospitality that the highlands are famous for." Her defence sounded weak even to her own ears! She knew she was over reacting, an open invitation to the incorrigible Jeannie.

"Of course he is one of nature's gentlemen, And the mere fact that you are the first woman invited out on a strictly personal basis for no less than fifteen years, would automatically lead a person to believe that it is his instinct to show Highland hospitality that prompted the invitation, and not the off chance that the gentlemen perhaps fancies your legs?" Sheer impish delight shone from Jeannie Campbell's eyes as she revelled in Linda's obvious embarrassment.

"Now, you stop that nonsense Jeannie. As if a woman of my age could take such silly notions seriously! I am bit long in the tooth to imagine for one moment that someone as sensible as Alan could ever harbour romantic notions about me. Absurd! The very idea is just too insane!" Her protest was rather too strong to sound convincing, even to her own ears, and she squirmed at her own patently obvious discomfort.

"Ahh. I see. Alan is too staid a man to look at you and feel the hot blood coursing through his veins! You worry me lassie. Have you forgotten you are a woman?

A very attractive one too, I may add! And what was that you said about your age? Surely you cannot think you are old?" Jeannie asked in bewilderment.

"Come on, Jeannie, I am no spring chicken. Anyone can see that. The very thought that romance is in the air indeed!"

"Good grief, lassie. You are just at your best and sexiest stage of your life! Have you ever taken a good look in the mirror? That is a real live honest to goodness flesh and blood female that you are seeing there, and that is exactly what Alan Ferguson sees when he looks at you. Not some old Methuselah! Ponder on this; he has invited you, Linda Cartell to accompany him tomorrow, because he wants a nice attractive female by his side. And remember this; Alan has always been renowned for his good taste!" Jeannie finished triumphantly.

Linda, now quite red in the face after listening to Jeannie's tirade, suddenly began to giggle. "I'll bet you that you get along famously with my Mum!" she said.

"As a matter of fact we did get on like a house on fire" she replied, puzzled.

"I just knew it! I have been listening to the same rhetoric for years Jeannie. Are you sure she was not on the phone giving you coaching lessons?"

"The very thought Mind you, if she had been, I would have completely agreed with her. I wasn't joking you know, you really are an attractive woman, and it's about time you were realising it, for your own good. Alan is too good a man to dismiss through your lack of self-confidence. You are surely not one of those women libbers, are you?"

"What? No." Linda replied, still giggling. "I have never been a women's Lib fan. I suppose that I have never met the right man, and therefore marriage has never entered the equation. My mum has never been able to understand that. She worries because I am an old maid in her eyes. When I listen to her for any length of time, mind you, I almost start to believe it myself!"

"Well, I guess that you will have to wear your tightest sweater tomorrow, and maybe give your Mum a nice wee surprise when you introduce your new husband at the end of your holiday. Tight sweaters have been known to work wonders you know!" Jeannie said in devilment.

"You really are incorrigible, Jeannie Campbell!" Linda retorted in good humour.

"One thing I have noticed, though, Jeannie. Alan has not got the same soft accent that you have. Do you come for a different area?"

"No. I was born and bred here. Alan and his brother went to boarding school, coming from the "monied" class of course. I am afraid it does not take the upper crust schools long to eradicate any trace of an accent from their pupils." She smiled as she thought back to other times. "I remember one summer when the boys came home for their holidays Alan telling his Dad about a teacher that overheard him singing an old sea shanty that my father had taught him to sing in Gaelic. Well! This teacher took him out in front of the class and said that he was making an example out of him as a lesson to the rest not to use that "heathen" tongue, and proceeded to administer six of the best with the cane! Poor wee soul, he was only seven!"

Jeannie shook her head then continued, "You would think that his father would have been outraged. Not him! All he said was "A spot of discipline is good for the soul, my lad", we were all amazed!

She smiled again as she said "I remember later that evening in the kitchen Alan whispering to me "A spot of discipline might be good for the soul, but it does not do the backside a lot of good, I'll tell you!"

Chapter Six

Linda was nursing a glass of German Brandy which she occasionally sipped, letting the golden liquid slip over her tongue slowly, and losing herself in the ambiance of the moment. She was sitting on an old wooden garden chair, enjoying the tranquillity of the evening.

A melodic bird call, which started on a low note and then sort of yodelled its way up the scale absolutely fascinated her, and she made a mental note to ask either Jeannie or Alan if they knew what bird it was. It was utterly delightful to listen to.

The sound of a car engine interrupted her reverie, and a few moments later, the now familiar Range Rover appeared over the horizon, and very soon stopped at the cottage.

"Good evening. I am on my way to home farm and I thought that it would do no harm to pop in and see how you are" Alan said with a broad smile on his handsome features.

"Thank you, kind sir" Linda replied, "I am delighted to have your company. Would you care for a little brandy?

It is quite unusual, from Germany. Not the usual French, but I find it very pleasant" Linda again felt the magnetic wonderfully blue eyes attracting her as she spoke.

"No thanks to the brandy, perhaps another time, but I wouldn't say no to a cup of coffee, if it is not too inconvenient? I never drink and drive." He said by way of explanation.

"I am sorry, I wasn't thinking. Coffee it is. You have impeccable timing; I just put the percolator on a short time ago. Would you care to come in to the kitchen, or would you prefer to sit out here?"

"It is such a lovely evening I think I prefer the garden. I always feel that it is tantamount to a sin to sit indoors in such beautiful weather. Make the most of it whilst it lasts, that's what I say."

"I would have questioned the wisdom of that just two days ago" Linda replied, "but now I can only agree with you whole heartedly."

"Amazing what a few days in the highlands can do, even to a born and bred "townie". You will be out rounding up the cattle in no time at all, now. Mark my words." Alan said jokingly.

"That will be the day!" Linda retorted as she went into the kitchen to fetch the coffee. A few moments later she emerged with a tray laden with sandwiches, scones (made by Jeannie) and a pot of piping hot Colombian coffee.

She had just started pouring the strong brown liquid in to the cup when the haunting sound of the same bird song came wafting through the air, quite unconsciously she stopped and stood perfectly motionless, enraptured by the sound.

"I think that is one of the most beautiful sounds I have ever heard. I have heard haunting bird calls in TV programmes, but I always assumed that there were sound effects added by engineers. That I am afraid is me. A born cynic. I am quite sure I probably owe David Attenborough and company an apology. Ignorance is a terrible cloak to wear, and I can see now that I cannot judge everything by the standards I have always adhered to the in the city." Linda said, kicking herself for rambling on again! Alan must think that she was nuts!

"What you are saying is that basically you only take at face value what you see on T.V. and read in the newspapers Most people share your view, I am afraid that the modern world, what with the technology that is used in the movie and television studios make it hard to determine what is real and what is fiction. He begins to feel that everything is a "con" job. Unfortunately, Mother Nature herself is rather adept at slight of hand also. You cannot believe at face value all you see or hear in nature to be true. Take the bird you heard just now, for example. Its song is really beautiful.The bird is a Curlew. Have you ever seen one?"

"No, I would not know a Curlew from a starling, it must be rather beautiful bird I would think. Something like a peacock I would imagine." She said.

"Well, it's not exactly a peacock" he replied, "in fact it is rather a drab brown, with a long curved bill, but it certainly has an exquisite song, especially compared to a peacock!" he laughed. "I promise to take you to the mud flats to see one. Now, what happened to that coffee?"

"I am sorry. I completely forgot that I was pouring it!" she said with embarrassment.

"No problem. I just thought that you were trying to starve me" he joked. "Regarding that bird. Nature gave the Curlew a terrific song, and one assumes that it must emanate from a beautiful bird. Humans tend to judge on either sight or sound and let the imagination run riot. The drab feathering of the curlew disappointments most people when they actually see one. Like real life, you cannot always believe what you see or hear in nature to be gospel, she is far too subtle for that. Sorry. I am going on a bit I must be boring you to tears."

"No, I am very interested. You know, I have lived my entire life in London, and I have never really understood what people find so special in country living. Not even in England's civilised rural pastures, let alone the wilds of northern Scotland. My eyes have been opened in a very short space of time, and I must admit that I find myself envious of you being able to live and work in such an idyllic place."

"I am glad that you like it. We all realise that we are very fortunate to live here. Perhaps that is why we are so passionate to protect the environment." Alan said in reply.

"Oh I am almost ashamed to admit that even when I have been abroad on holidays, I have stuck to the cities like glue. To me, that was the way to really see and experience a country. I believed that if one could sense the sophistication of the pace, then one really experienced the real essence of that country. How wrong can one be! I have never before even contemplated life without the excitement of career and success, money and all it brings, and sheer tension of business stress to keep the adrenaline pumping at full throttle. Even the experience of failure has its own nerve tingling excitement in its own fashion. That is city life, and I honestly believed until now the only life worth having. The country was for hicks, no insult intended, and to be totally honest, I argued with my mother rather intently before agreeing to come here. Boy! Now am I grateful to her. Oh dear, it's me that seems to be going on a bit now." She said.

"Nonsense. I am enjoying listening to you, I find it very interesting. Please do continue" Alan said sincerely. He nursed his coffee, admiring Linda. The passion in her husky contralto voice matched the intensity of feeling in her eyes, and he was quite content to listen, study her beautiful face, and let her voice envelop him in richly woven fabric of sound. It was like being wrapped in a tapestry of oral velvet, he mused.

"I only agreed to come here to placate my mother, knowing quite well that I would detest every minute spent away from the city. Now I find myself in the strange position for the first time in my life that right at this moment, I couldn't care less if I ever saw the city again! Not only am I surrounded by beauty, but I am totally relaxed for the first time since I was a child, and it is a marvellous feeling! That is a completely new experience for me, and I love it!" she said with exuberance.

"I am pleased for you, Linda. Relaxation is a very precious commodity these days." Alan observed.

"I still have my problems, of course, but they seem to have shrunk in their significance. I am totally at ease with my inner self, and my self confidence has returned in a very short space of time. I know that success will be mine, no matter what opportunity presents itself in the future, even if it far removed form the only business I really know, I now realize that it would not mean the end of the world." She smiled at Alan, her emotional equilibrium now fully restored.

"The highlands have a calming quality which I have never found anywhere else in the world" he said, and whenever I have been away on business, which is as seldom as possible, I tend to get uptight, and I can't wait to return home."

Linda smiled as she replenished his coffee. "You are a very fortunate man to not only live in a place that you love, but actually be able to run your business from home and avoid the stresses of commuting to and fro each and everyday. No traffic worries or pollution, or the myriad of other problems that the city dweller has to contend with, and may I add that I don't think that there is much chance of your being mugged up here!" she quipped.

Alan chuckled and said, "I don't think your average mugger would dare to pass the highland cattle up in the glen. So I think we are fairly safe right enough."

"I had forgotten about them!" she said, and they both laughed loudly.

"You must find running the estate very fulfilling, it must almost feel like you are running your own little country" she paused, and the giggled. "Just had a thought, I suppose it is akin to having your own little kingdom, so you are the nearest thing to royalty I shall ever meet" she said, and curtsied very respectfully.

Alan burst out laughing. "Well, I see that the lady doth have a sense of humour. I therefore hereby grant thee the freedom of the glen, and the royal approval to pet all cattle within its borders."

"That is one honour I think I shall forego" she replied with a good humour.

"The truth is that there is so much legislation pouring out from Brussels and London, about the only decision that is left entirely in my hands is what time to have breakfast" he explained in a more serious tone.

"Surely it cannot be as bad as that. A slight exaggeration, perhaps?"

"Just ask any farmer in Britain, and if the reply isn't the same, I'll eat my hat. I manage to beat the sheer frustration of idiotic bureaucracy that has that has been thrust upon of the agricultural community, by taking an interest in other lines of business, far removed from agriculture. The freedom to use my brain and skills, such as I have, is a delight to be savoured. Honestly." He held his hand in the boy scouts salute.

"I never realised that things were so frustrating for farmers. One thing I do know is that whatever else you have an active interest in can only benefit from your involvement." Linda answered.

"Thank you, kind lady. Diversification has proved to be the best thing I have done. It affords me a freedom of choice long since taken from the farmer. At least if I make a bad decision, it is my mistake, and that is the spur that drives me, in all honesty, and not the financial gain, although very few people would believe that."

"I believe you Alan" Linda said "I have no idea what interests you have out with the estate, or how much money you may earn from them, but no matter what the sum, I am positive that what you have told me is truth and that being able to exercise the freedom of choice is by far the most important factor."

"I appreciate that very much Linda. By the way, speaking of freedom of choice, I am going to a couple of fish farms tomorrow. I don't think I actually told you where we would be going, did I?"

"No you didn't actually" Linda replied, not too sure now if she had been too hasty in to agreeing to go.

"Sorry about that. As I was saying, we go to the fish farms, and then we'll have a spot of lunch. Now unfortunately, I have had to change my plans slightly, I must go to Glasgow in the afternoon, which is rather a drag, but I was wondering if perhaps you would consider coming? Glasgow has some fabulous shops, and I am sure you would find the change of pace refreshing. One thing before you reply" he cautioned, "We shall have to stay overnight, as I have a breakfast meeting at six thirty the next morning. I promise I'll be finished by the eight, the gentleman I am meeting wit h catches his flight at seven forty, so I'll definitely be free by eight. I thought we could then make a day of it touring the city before returning home."

"Are you propositioning me, Alan Ferguson? Linda questioned rather mischievously.

"No! No! Please don't misunderstand. I just thought that maybe you would be glad of a wee change!" he blurted anxiously.

"I was only joking" she laughed. "Just thought I would get some of my own back" she gloated. "I would love to come, Alan. Who knows, perhaps I have secret designs on you? You may be the one to have second thoughts before morning" she said teasingly.

"Well! I had better remember to splash on the old aftershave. I hear that you women prefer it to the aroma that usually permeates around a country hick like myself" he quipped.

"How very perceptive, my good man. Oh yes, and please remember to remove the strand of straw from your teeth when we get to the big city!" she was amazed at her own audacity!

"Yes, m'lady. oi'll try to remember. Perhaps would be so kind as to 'old moi' and when we gets to them there traffic lights Oi as 'eard of then?" He replied in his best impression of 'Walter Gabrial' from the 'Archers' radio programme.

"I promise that I won't let go of your hand all the time we are in the big bad city" she said, patting his head as she spoke, joining in the mood of the moment.

"Thank 'ee, ma'am, Oi'll 'old thee to that on the 'morrow'." He laughed.

"By the way, you never said what time we are leaving in the morning" Linda said with trepidation, imagining a very early start.

"Relax." Alan said, noticing her concern. "We don't have to leave till nine or so." Her relief would have been obvious even to a blind man" he mused.

"That suits me fine. I had terrible visions of having to rise in the middle of night."

"You are sure that you do really want to come, and that you don't feel pressured by me?"

"Honestly, Alan, I would love to come with you and anyway, how on earth would you ever manage at the traffic lights in Glasgow without me?" she bantered.

"Then Oi'll be taking moi leave of thee then, moi lady. Till the morrow" he said, kissing her hand, taking her totally by surprise!

"I'll wish you a very good night then, my good fellow" she said, continuing the joke. "Thank you for your company and please don't lie awake all night worrying about the big city. I promise I will look after you." They were still laughing as he pulled the Range Rover onto the road. He blew the horn and waved as he went over the crest of the hill on his way to home farm.

Bright sunshine greeted Linda as she stepped into the garden on hearing the now familiar sound of Alan's car approaching. She was wearing sensible flat shoes, denims and a plaid shit, and a short suede jacket. She has spent a little extra time over her make up (much to her own bemusement) and was almost startled to find her heart give a little flutter when the car same in to view.

"Get a grip of yourself, you silly female" she muttered out loud as she picked up the small valise she had packed for the overnight stay in Glasgow.

The morning flew past n a glorious montage of mountains and lochs, and wonderful glimpses of those amazing blue eyes!

A small family-owned hotel which Alan said he often dined, provided them with a luncheon menu which would have given any London eating establishment more than a run for its money.

Linda eventually decided upon grilled salmon set on a bed of courgettes, followed by a delicious poached pear smothered in a rich chocolate sauce dessert, having been persuaded by her companion to indulge herself. Undoubtedly extremely fattening, but how wickedly delicious!

"I have heard that food is the way to a man's heart, but'll have to confess that you have found the perfect weapon to this particular girl's heart" she joked. "The meal was simply scrumptious!"

"Well, now I have discovered your weakness, I can't possibly go wrong. When you savour dinner in Glasgow tonight you will be as putty in my hands, I'll try to remember that I am a gentleman, and refrain from ordering extra dessert just to have my wicked way with you!" he laughed.

Please don't try too hard, she thought longingly, losing herself in a reverie of blue eyes and dreamt of kisses.

Back in the car, Linda was surprised to find Alan leave the main road and head along a single track that appeared to be going back into the "wilds" rather than towards Inverness as she had envisaged the route would be. When she asked him if this was a short cut he burst out laughing!

"In a sense I suppose it is a kind of short cut. Didn't I tell you, we are flying?!"

Chapter Seven

The plane was an eight seater twin engine turbo prop, which was sitting on a private runway waiting for them. Linda was completely astounded to discover Alan owned it! The pilot was Dick Hays, a tall lanky individual with a permanent smile on his face. Alan explained he held his own pilots licence, but it was only for single engine craft.

"I thought you farmers could hardly afford a bicycle these days, how on earth can you afford this? Oh, I am sorry Alan that was extremely ignorant of me. It is none of my business, and I do apologise." Her face reddened brightly, and she could have died on the spot!

Alan laughed aloud and said "Please don't apologise, my dear Linda. The farm couldn't pay for the fuel for this thing, let alone buy it. My other interests provide the wherewithal, and very glad I am too. I really should have told you that it was my aircraft we would be flying in, so I apologise to you" He smiled broadly, and gave her hand a friendly squeeze.

Linda, now put at ease by Alan, thoroughly enjoyed the flight. Both Alan and Dick pointed out the endless lochs by name, plus the seemingly endless mountains, all named Ben this or Ben that, all incomprehensive to her. They both regaled her with stories of Bonnie Prince Charlie, which she wasn't sure whether to believe or not! Both men swore every word was true!

A limousine was waiting at the airport, and quickly whisked them to an exclusive hotel about fifteen miles from Glasgow. Alan arranged to meet her in the lounge bar once she had freshened up.

There was no doubt about it, she mused as she enjoyed a welcome hot shower, Alan Ferguson was indeed a man of surprises and a certain amount of mystery! He was obviously extremely successful, but just what was his business?

Alan was seated at the corner table of the bar when she entered, and he smiled broadly and said "I hope you don't mind, I have taken the liberty to order a brandy for you?"

"Thank you kind sir, a brandy is excellent. I am glad I came, I have had a most enjoyable and surprising day, thank you"

"I am delighted to hear it. But what you actually should have said is that you have had a most enjoyable day, SO FAR."

"Now your intriguing me, just what surprise so you have in store for me now, Alan Ferguson?"

"Well, dinner first, then we....no, why don't we just let it happen? Just go with the flow?"

Linda looked at him, and then shrugged. "Why not? Let's go with the flow, man."

"Right on baby!" he said, "let the good times roll." In an excellent New York accent.

"You really are incorrigible. No, that is not quite the word, more…."

"Infuriating?" he proffered.

"Yes. Infuriating! But I may add also exceedingly charming…at times." She smiled and touched his hand.

He held up his glass and said "Cheers, Linda Cartell" and she melted into those dangerous blue eyes.

Linda relaxed happily in the rear of the Daimler limousine, resting her arm on the leather arm rest, unconsciously clasping Alan's hand. The car sped along as they chatted, and she was surprised when it drew to a stop, and she found they were in front of a small village hall.

Looking at Alan she said that when he had said let the good times roll she was expecting a rather pretentious night club in Glasgow or even Edinburgh, filled with the parochial "in" crowd. But a tiny village hall!!

"Well, I figured if we went to a club, it would seem no different to London, so I decided upon something quite entirely parochial. We are going to a Ceiladh!"

"A what?"

"A Ceiladh. A sort of dinner dance, only more of a party really. I promise that if you don't have a great time, I will take you to any venue you care to name, anywhere in the world! Word of honour. He held his hand up in the boy scouts salute, and grinned widely.

"Any place in the entire world?" she said in astonishment.

"In the whole world, I promise"

"You really are extraordinary! And certainly full of surprises…Or, come to think of it, just pain nuts." She giggled.

"There is only one way to find out. Let's go to the Ceiladh!" He wrapped his arm around her waist, and steered into Auchen Village Hall.

His supreme self confidence was of course well justified, Linda had the most fun she had ever had in her entire life! A band comprising of two accordions, a fiddle, double bass a piano and drums, filled the tiny stage at the far end of the hall. They played reels, jigs, waltzes and square dances non stop until midnight.

Everyone then dug in to a delicious buffet with as much gusto as they had put into their dancing! Linda amazed herself at how much she ate, enjoying every mouthful to the last morsel. Then, the whole thing started all over again! The floorboards vibrated by stamping feet as the dancers whirled and stepped with renewed energy.

The hall spun around as she was passed from partner to partner in an eight some reel, and then gently but firmly in Alan's arms for a waltz, only to be spun and whirled once more in a Gay Gordons.

And so the night melted away in an amazing mosaic of music, dance, food, and the comfort of Alan's arms. She now new beyond any doubt what she had known from the instant she had met him, but had refused to admit to herself, she was madly in love with Alan Ferguson!

This tall handsome Scot with the magnetic blue eyes had stolen her heart. The impossible had happened, for the first time in her life, she was really, truly, honestly, in love! And with a man who hadn't even kissed her, she remembered!

She smiled to herself as she held his hand tightly. "The height of absurdity" she would have said, if her mother had told her such feelings for a man were possible that she was now experiencing. But what utterly glorious feelings!

"Well, where is it going to be?" the sound of Alan's voice snapped her back to reality.

"Sorry Alan, I was in a dream"

"I said where it will be? I did offer to take you anywhere in the world, remember?"

"Oh Alan, I had a fabulous evening, and the only place on this world I want to be is right here, where I am with you. Thank you for a wonderful time. She gave his hand an affectionate squeeze as she spoke.

"Thank you kind lady" he replied, and I am exactly where I want to be too" and pulling her closer, he looked deeply into her eyes, and kissed her tenderly on the lips.

Dawn was breaking as the car pulled up in front of their hotel. Linda felt as though she was walking on air as they made there way to the foyer. Her lip still pulsated with his kiss, and she longed for this night to go on for ever.

"I have a meeting first thing in the morning, and I am quite sure you will want to rest. The car is at your disposal all morning, and the driver will take you sight seeing or shopping if you wish. He smiled as they reached her room, cupped her chin in his hand and kissed her gently. "Thank you for a wonderful evening, Linda. I enjoyed it immensely. I'll call on the car phone when the meeting is over. Goodnight, dear." His lips caressed hers once more, and then he was gone.

Having slept soundly for five hours, Linda woke feeling as fresh as a daisy. After a shower, she went to the dining room. Normally she had toast and marmalade with a cup of coffee for breakfast, but this morning she found herself ordering bacon, eggs, black pudding and fried potatoes, with a rack of toast and a pot of coffee.

Visions of dancing into the wee small hours, and the lingering sweetness of Alan's kisses filled her mind as she enjoyed another coffee and a cigarette. She had no idea at that moment in time what the future held in store for her, but one thing she did know for certain, life would never be the same again.

Leaving the dinner room she was greeted by William, the chauffeur who had driven them the previous evening.

"Good morning, Miss. I trust had an enjoyable breakfast? Mr Ferguson instructed me to take you where ever you wish. He telephoned a short while ago. I have to apologise on his behalf, unfortunately his meeting is taking longer that anticipated, and he asked if you can meet him at the La Continental restaurant around one for lunch?"

"I shall certainly meet him as long as you know where the restaurant is, William, she said with a mischievous twinkle in her eye.

"I am sure I can locate the establishment, Miss. Now where can I take you in the interim?"

"You know. I honestly don't know where to go. I am not familiar with the area. I am at rather a loss. Where would you suggest?"

"Would you care for the shops in Glasgow, or perhaps a run in the car to Loch Lomond?" he kindly suggested.

"I would love to see Loch Lomond, but isn't it too far to be able to keep my appointment at one?" she asked.

"Och, we have ample time, Miss. The Loch is only about twelve miles form here, he said, giving her a friendly smile. He then escorted Linda to a beautiful navy blue Ford Scorpio Granada, and held open the rear door for her.

She hesitated a moment, and then said "Would you wind if I sat in front seat, or are you not allowed to carry a passenger in the front?"

"Of course you can ride in the front Miss" he replied amiably, and dutifully opened the front passenger door.

"Thank you William, I shall enjoy the drive a lot more sitting in the front of the car, perhaps because invariably I am usually driving myself. I tend to find the rear a bit intimidating when I am on my own."

She found the run to Loch Lomond to be a pleasure, the scenery was beautiful, but although this was her first time there, it all seemed strangely familiar. When William explained that the T.V. soap opera "Take the High Road" was filmed on the loch side, she at once understood its familiarity; she had been a fan of the series for years.

They had coffee in the village of Luss, where most of the soap is filmed, and she had to admire the way the indigenous entrepreneurs pumped the T.V. connection for every penny that they could. The tourists loved it! She purchased some post cards and a few souvenirs in the village, and all in all she had a very relaxing morning.

Alan was seated at his table when she arrived at the restaurant. He greeted her with a huge smile, and asked if she had enjoyed her morning.

"I have had a wonderful morning, thank you, and William was most informative. I now know all about

Loch Lomond, and the T.V. series filmed there, and I have been regaled with Rob Roy Mcgregor's exploits in the area back in the era of the clans."

"I am glad William kept you entertained, he is a great character. I always try to have his services when I am down here." Alan told her.

Lunch was excellent, and they were lingering over their coffee, when the owner came and informed Alan very discreetly that the press had gathered outside the restaurant.

"I fear that word had leaked out that you are dining here, I do hope this won't inconvenience you too much, Alan." He said.

"I would rather sidestep the media at this particular point in time Robert. Got any suggestions?" Alan asked.

"Yes, I think I may be able to help, let's go to my office. I have a private lift from it to the roof, the management car park is built on it. You are most welcome to the use of my car, Alan, if it is of any help."

"You are a life saver, Robert. I promise the car shall be returned within an hour." He replied gratefully. They followed Robert to his office, and then proceeded to the roof.

"Thanks again, Robert. I won't forget this" Alan said as he and Linda got into the car.

"All part of the service, old boy. The ramp comes out onto Mitchell Lane, I am sure the press won't be looking for you there." Robert said.

"I am sure you are right. Can I ask for another favour, Robert? Would you please inform William what has happened, and tell him to give me a five minute start, and then he can lead them a merry chase!"

"Count it done, Alan. I look forward to seeing you soon, and it was a pleasure meeting you, Linda"

"I promise it won't be long before we return, and next time I hope we don't have to make such a dramatic departure!" Alan replied as he closed the car door.

Linda sat in the borrowed car, rather bewildered by the hasty back door exit they ad just made. Why on earth would the press be so interested in Alan?

Robert's prediction proved correct. There was no sign if the press when the car entered the street. As they turned onto the main street, she saw hordes of photographers and TV crews outside the restaurant doors, waiting like a flock of vultures. Alas, in vein, she mused.

"Sorry about the cloak and dagger but, but I avoid the media like the plague, I am afraid'. Alan explained apologetically.

"Don't worry about it. In fact I feel as though I am in a spy movie. Are you sure you are not really James Bond?" she teased. "Only a little minor point, really, why are the press so interested in Alan Ferguson?"

"I do owe you an explanation. It is quite simple, actually. One of my companies is in the throes of making a take over bid for a larger enterprise, and I guess that the press has sussed it out, so that makes me news worthy I reckon" he said matter of factly.

"One thing is for sure, life is certainly never dull or boring around you, Alan Ferguson!" she laughed.

"On the subject of business, I am afraid that I have been forced to change our itinerary rather drastically, due to technical legality. I must fly to Canada, today! He announced. "Dick will of course fly you back to the estate. I know I am leaving you in the lurch, and I am sorry. I do hope you understand. I don't really have a choice in the matter" he glanced at her with those dark blue eyes, and at that moment she would have walked back to the highlands on her hands if he had asked her!

"Business must come first Alan. No argument. I do understand, and no offence is taken. I would like to know if you have any idea how long you are likely to be away for?"

"That is extremely difficult to answer. A few days only, I hope. Maybe as long as a week." He replied.

"Oh. I see." She could not disguise her disappointment.

"Listen, I don't suppose you would have your passport with you?" he blurted.

"Actually, I do have it in my handbag. I always feel that is the safest place for it. Why?"

"I know this will sound crazy, but I want you to come to Vancouver with me."

"What? You surely are not serious? How can I fly off to Canada just like that? I haven't even any luggage. The few overnight things I brought to Glasgow are in the hotel, and I would require a lot more than that if I was going to the other side of the Atlantic." She protested.

"A trivial matter. You can purchase all your requirements in Vancouver. You have your passport, you have all you need. Please, say that you'll come."

"You are quite mad, Alan Ferguson. Even if I did agree to come, it is highly unlikely that I could get a seat at this late hour. Be practical." She said.

"If I guarantee to secure a seat on the plane for you, will you agree to accompany me, then?"

"You have persuaded me, I'll come with you. But I cannot see you managing to get a seat for me." She was relieved beyond belief that if he could secure her a seat, she would not be parted from him for even a moment, but did not want to say so. But she was positive that even he would not secure a seat on the aircraft.

"Fantastic! I have confession to make. I love you, Linda Cartell, and I don't want to be apart from you." She was astounded!

"I..I..what did you say?"

"I said I love you, and I am probably even more astonished than you are. I never thought I would ever say those words to anyone again. But I am sincere, I do love you Linda." He said with feeling.

"Oh, Alan, I love you too. I have since the moment we met, and I have been fighting my feelings ever since. We got off to such a bad start. I thought you would never be able to love me."

"You are silly Linda. I love you and you love me, what else matters?" he took her hand in his and kissed it. A few moments later they drove into Glasgow airport.

Much to her surprise, they did not go into the car park, but carried on to the cargo terminal. "Don't tell me you are shipping me out as freight?" she quipped.

"Mmm…something like that." He answered, winking mischievously at her. A moment later they pulled up on front of a pristine white executive jet!" I have consulted the owner, and he assures me there is a spare seat." He beamed at her.

"But you haven't spoken to anyone except me. How can you have asked the owner?" Her mouth suddenly gaped open in disbelief. "You are the owner!" she said as the obvious dawned. "You have taken my breath away. I never expected anything like this, it is absolutely beautiful" she said in admiration as she looked at the sleek gleaming aircraft.

"You ain't seen nothing yet, gal, as they say in the movies" he said in a perfect Texan drawl.

"I can believe that. I don't think anything could ever surprise me again." She whispered.

Chapter Eight

Soft warm raindrops caressed Linda's cheeks as she strolled aimlessly along the pebble beach. A small tug boat was towing a gigantic raft of huge logs southward to meet their ultimate destiny in the saw mills of Vancouver.

She paused to watch the tiny craft pull its vast burden through the deep waters of Lions Bay. The awesome power the small boat had to be able to tow hundreds of trees weighing goodness only knew how many tonnes, amazed her. She smiled to herself. This display of raw power somehow seemed to her to epitomise the power which Alan seemed to command, effortlessly.

The only difference she could discern, was that the tug's engines throbbed loudly, undoubtedly being driven to their limits, whereas Alan was always unruffled, giving the impression of being well within himself, confident of his own capabilities. He exuded authority with the air of a general, but invariably with the grace of a pope. Linda did not know how he managed it. He was truly amazing, she thought. They had been in Canada for eight days now, and she still had to pinch herself to make certain that she wasn't dreaming. Time and events had passed with such alacrity that it literally made her head spin.

How long had it been since her Mum had cajoled her into going to Scotland? So many things had transpired since, and she found it almost impossible to believe that it was less than a month!

Inevitably, her thoughts returned to Alan. That tall handsome country yokel, as she had assumed him to be on their initial meeting. Boy! Some yokel he had turned out to be!

On the flight from Glasgow, he had talked incessantly. At first about business, explaining the trip to Vancouver was essential to finalize the take-over of a television satellite network! She was utterly staggered! He explained that Canadian regulations required his being there in person, or the deal would not be ratified by the Canadian government. "Typical red tape nonsense." He commented.

Linda found to her surprise that Alan had explained the situation so matter of fact, that she just accepted the whole scenario an everyday occurrence, like it was no big deal to go out and buy a TV satellite network!

When she asked him how he could remain so calm, he just smiled and replied "I have you." She looked at him and said it was very flattering of him to say so, but he was obviously a businessman of some repute in Scotland, who went to extreme lengths to avoid publicity. What on earth was he going to do now if he succeeded in this bid? Instead of being a reluctant celebrity living in the remote highlands, this would make him a player on the world stage, and there was no possibility of remaining anonymous then!

Taking her hand in his he squeezed affectionately, and said "Thank you, my darling. I thought that you were going to tell me that I was probably biting off more that I can chew, perhaps pushing my luck too regarding my business expertise? My happiness was your prime concern, and that makes me very glad indeed." He pulled her closer to him and kissed her tenderly.

"I never doubted your ability or business acumen, I am just worried about the publicity this is bound to generate" she replied, "I know how you hate it."

"Darling Linda, there are some things I must explain to you. When you said that this venture would thrust me upon the world stage and make me a world player, I think you said? To be totally honest, I have used the obscurity of the estate for quite some time now. I have never really thought of myself in the context of being a world player before, but on reflection, I guess I actually am, and have been for a considerable period. Quite a number of years in, fact."

"You surely mean that you have interests out with Britain, Alan. But I hardly think that qualifies you into the league of the world business moguls. I am not trying to demean you, darling. But you told me yourself that the company you are currently vying to buy is larger than your own. Obviously the media circus will be in attendance, and I don't know if you fully realise what that will mean for you. I am afraid that the sanctity of the estate won't save you from a lifetime of scrutiny that

I doubt if you can accept." Linda looked lovingly but seriously at him.

"I appreciate your concern my dear. It is true that International Satellite Systems is much larger that the company that launched the take-over bid, but what I did not fully explain is that particular company in turn is a subsidiary of a far larger concern. Perhaps you have heard of the Alan Arnold Group?"

"Oh, my darling Alan, please be careful. I have heard of the Alan Arnold Group. Indeed I have!" Linda said bitterly.

"What on earth is so terrible about the Alan Arnold Group?"

Linda explained her boardroom battles with Sir Geoffrey, and her eventual demise, and indeed the total capitulation of the entire board as they succumbed to the pressure applied by Sir Geoffrey on behalf of the Alan Arnold Group, the company that was headed by the infamous (in her opinion) Alan Arnold!

"London Residential," he said thoughtfully, "if my memory serves me correctly, after the take-over and the necessary rationalisation, the new stronger company is going extremely well, the threat of bankruptcy in a very depressed market is now a thing of the past. Not only that, my dear Linda, but over eighty percent of those who lost their positions, however regrettable at the time, not only collected an average payment of seventeen thousand pounds, but have since been given alternative employment within the Alan Arnold Group. The others either found other positions elsewhere or chose to retire.

Now does the infamous Alan Arnold still seem such a terrible person to you?"

"Obviously in the light of what you have said, the answer is no. I have never heard these facts. But how come you are so well informed, Alan?" she queried.

"Mmm. It is a long story but I'll try to explain"

"Please do. I am intrigued." She said expectantly.

"Well, it seems like a lifetime ago now. After my father died, my brother and I were faced with massive death duties, and the estate simply did not generate the income to pay them. After much deliberation, we decided to invest our meagre resources into areas out with the estate. Fortunately father had had the foresight to educate his sons at St.Andrews University, where we both took degrees in Business Management. So at least we both had the qualifications, if not adequate capital."

He suddenly laughed. "All that education and grand theory, and of course the first thing we did, naturally we made a complete mess of!"

Linda listened intently, engrossed in his every word.

"We decided the first step was to form a limited company. After a few ideas were kicked around we eventually decided on a name for this company. Alan and Arnold. Limited. Unfortunately, when Arnold filled out the registration form, he wrote Alan Arnold in error!"

Linda gasped at him in astonishment! "You are Alan Arnold!"

"In actual fact, as I have just explained, there is in fact, no such person, he smiled. Fortunately, no one from the media has done their homework properly. They have always assumed that Alan Arnold exists. Worked out perfectly for me!" he beamed.

"How on earth have you managed to sustain the myth for so long?" she asked. "I am amazed to put it mildly."

"By various means. Arnold was killed in an air crash before the company was big enough to attract the attention of the press. I guess it was the take-over of the Continental Hotel chain that first sparked their interest. For some unexplained reason they assumed that Alan Arnold was the power behind the scenes, you know, a mysterious figure in a grey suit. I have never felt the urge to correct the error." He smiled broadly, cupped her face in his hands, and kissed her.

"Do you still love me, or now that you know that I am the infamous Alan Arnold does it mean the end?"

"Of course I still love you, you idiot! She said, and returned his kiss passionately.

The rest of the flight passed very quickly for Linda, as Alan explained how he ran the business from the estate with just a few key staff. They lived and worked in the mansion, and got extended holidays to compensate for their isolation. The company had hotels worldwide, and staff at the estate got free accommodation and flights twice yearly. Alan's accommodation was the top floor of the mansion. The house had fifty six rooms. Enough to go around." He stated.

"My right hand man is Bret Gray, did you meet him, by any chance?" he asked Linda.

"No. I was involved in boardroom discussions, of course, but direct contact with Alan Arnold group was carried out by Sir Geoffrey" she replied.

"Well, you'll have the pleasure of meeting him shortly, he is already in Vancouver." Alan told her.

Bret Gray was waiting at the airport, with of course, a limousine. To Linda's surprise and delight, the first thing on the agenda was to proceed to the nearest shopping mall, to enable her to buy a whole new wardrobe! Alan insisted buying her purchases, despite her protests.

They then proceeded northeast from the city to Lions Bay, where Alan had a beautiful house built a few years before, overlooking the beautiful tidal bay Linda had ever seen. They went for a walk along the shore, and the sea breeze was very refreshing after the long flight from Scotland. Alan slipped his arm around her waist, and she snuggled in closely to him, tired but happy.

They paused to watch a sea lion as it dived from the rock it was lying on, entering the water without leaving a ripple, only to surface again only a few yards from them quite unperturbed by there presence. This was the first sea lion Linda had ever seen, and she was fascinated.

She asked Alan if the bay was named after the sea lions, and almost had a fit when he replied that the bay was in fact named Lions Bay after the mountain lions which live there, also known as cougars.

"Mountain lions! Are you teasing me again, Alan Ferguson?" she asked, hoping fervently that he was.

"No. It is perfectly true, my dear, but don't get up tight. There seems to be very few of them about nowadays, too much human activity for their liking."

"Thank goodness for that," he said with relief, "from a personal perspective, of course, but a shame for the lions, all the same." She said with sympathy.

"I am sure the mountain lions would agree with the latter sentiment entirely. Oh, on the subject of agreeing, there is something I was wondering if you would agree to before I get submerged in business negotiations." He stopped walking and looked deeply into her eyes.

She waited in anticipation. He paused for a few seconds, and then said "Will you marry me Linda?"

She gazed into those wonderful blue eyes, and immediately whispered, "Yes, my darling Alan, yes!" and they embraced passionately.

That night Linda lay in bed in deep thought. Alan was the man of her dreams, and she loved him dearly, and she had just agreed to marry him. She should have been the happiest woman in the world. But a secret, a terrible secret that only her mother and she had shared, had now returned to haunt her with a vengeance!

What to do? She lay awake for hours, her mind in a turmoil. She knew she should, indeed must, tell Alan, but would he then despise her and spurn her? She loved him as she had never loved before, and it was tearing her apart. Dare she risk all by telling him? She cried herself to sleep.

The following morning she resolved she must confess to Alan and tell him why she could not marry him. No matter how strong her love, she new that she could never wed such a fine man, it was breaking her heart!

But somehow, between business meetings, business lunches and business dinners followed by even more endless business meetings, the days had flown past, and the few brief moments that they had had together, Linda's courage had failed her, and so she kept her secret, feeling ever guilty and ever more miserable!

Now, as she strolled along the shore, rain soaked and thoroughly ashamed of herself for having been so cowardly, she wept silently as she recalled and deeply regretted the most shameful episode of her life.

The excuses she had made to herself over the last few weeks were now long past their sell by date. Her heart sank to the soles of her feet. No more excuses were possible now. Alan and Bret had just completed their negotiations successfully for the acquisition of the TV Satellite Company.

She aimlessly kicked a pebble and watched as it rolled down the beach and splashed into the water. "Like that little stone, you too must take the plunge, my girl." She said aloud as she heard the sound of the Lincoln Continental limousine return from Vancouver. She was at the lowest ebb of her life!

Alan and Bret arrived in jubilant mood, elated with the successful outcome of their hard fought negotiations. Alan immediately asked the housekeeper where Linda was, he donned a waterproof jacket and went to the beach to fetch her to join in the celebrations.

Linda had been a tower of patience and strength over the period, never once complaining when he and Bret frequently had to work into the wee small hours. She always had a smile for him, words of encouragement and a welcome drink just at the right moment. Now he would make amends. Take the time to make proper wedding arrangements with her, and commit himself to give Linda the lion's share of his time for the rest of his life, he vowed to himself.

He hurried down the footpath to the shore, ignoring the rain which had gotten even heavier, his heart full of love and happiness for this beautiful woman. Linda was at the waters edge, and he ran and swept her into his arms and kissed her passionately.

"I have so much to tell you, my darling, but first we had better return to the house out of this rain" he said, noticing that her auburn hair was soaked through.

"Alan, my love, my life. Please sit on this rock. I have something I must tell you, and my courage may fail me if we if we go indoors. Please, my darling, please sit on the rock and hear me out" she looked at him pleadingly, and he could see panic in her eyes.

"What on earth is wrong darling, it can't be that bad surely?" trying to smile. Linda suddenly burst into tears, sobbing uncontrollably.

Alan held her tightly to him, trying to console her. Please tell me what is the matter darling. Take your time and tell me. Please!" he implored.

"Oh, Alan, I love you with all my heart. You must believe m.m.m.e." she stammered between sobs.

"Of course I believe you" he said, holding her even more tightly to home. "Whatever makes you think that I would not?" He could feel her heart pounding against her breast.

"I have a dreadful secret to tell you. I love you with my entire being Alan. But I cannot marry you!!" she exclaimed dramatically.

Chapter Nine

Alan looked at Linda in utter disbelief! What on earth had happened to make her say that she loved him so, but could not marry him?

He held her even more tightly to him, trying to console her. No matter what the problem was, he loved this woman, and vowed that they would be married, no matter what this secret, and pity help man or beast that tried to prevent him!

Ever so slowly, her sobs began to subside, as she responded to Alan's caresses. She wanted so desperately to kiss him, but daren't. She knew that she was not worthy of this noble and gentle man.

"Come on darling. Nothing in this life is ever as bad as it may seem. Everything can be worked out, given time, you'll see" he said soothingly.

"If only that where true Alan. Oh, how I wish that!" she said tearfully.

Ignoring the rain, which was now pouring heavily, he cupped her face in his powerful hands, and kissed her gently on the lips. "Now, dry your tears, my dearest, and tell me what has transpired to upset you so." He kissed her tenderly on the cheek.

Linda composed herself, and then began: I will tell you, Alan, but first I want you to promise that you will hear me out without interrupting me. Please promise." He gave her his solemn word, stroking her hair all the while, trying to relax her.

Linda averted his eyes, and stared transfixed at the stony beach. "This is the most difficult thing I have ever had to do, Alan, because I am going to hurt you very deeply with what I am thoroughly ashamed of myself for having been too much of a coward for not telling you before. Also I love you too much, and clung on to the dream that it was possible to marry you for as long as I could, and it was very wrong of me. I hope you can find it in your heart to forgive me that when I have finished." She paused for a second to gather herself.

"I don't deserve to be your wife" she began, and held her finger to his lips when he made to protest. "You promised to hear me out" he remained silent. "I made a mistake an extremely bad mistake a long time ago, and I have had to live with the guilt ever since. When I was young, I fell madly in love, at least I thought it was love at the time, but it was a foolish infatuation. He was a bit of a tearaway, and he rode a big fast motorbike. Being a silly teenager, who had led a very sheltered life, I was really impressed. I am not sure now whether by him or the bike. My parents were appalled when they met him, and immediately barred me from seeing him again. Needless to say, that was like a red rag to a bull! We had a furious row, and I left home and school, to live with my swashbuckling motorbike hero."

She took a deep breath, and then continued. "Two months later, Stuart, his name was Stuart Wilson, was killed on the bike, coming home from a drinking session with his friends. His death was a terrible shock at the time, but after two months of perpetual beatings and his drunkenness, I was to be honest more relieved than saddened. What was the real tragedy for me was that I discovered that I was pregnant!"

Linda looked extremely forlorn as she attempted to light a cigarette, but her hand was shaking so much that she was finding it impossible to connect the flame from the lighter to the end of the cigarette. Alan gently took the lighter and held it steady in front of her.

"Thank you" she said gratefully as she inhaled deeply. "I know, I should have given this habit up years ago, but it is a comfort." Alan stroked her hair all the while, saying nothing, his heart breaking for his beautiful Linda.

"When the funeral was over I didn't know what to do. I was panic stricken. Alan, living in a rented room in Brighton, too terrified to phone my parents which common sense told me was the correct and sensible thing to do, but what sense I possessed had long since deserted me.

"I just couldn't think" she took a long pull on her cigarette.

"I sent the summer season working as a waitress, living in my furnished room in abject misery. I hated morning sickness, and my swollen tummy. I was really very depressed and very confused." She sat with a fixed stare, her head bowed in shame.

"I lost my job at the end of the season, and spent weeks sitting in my room, living in a daze. Then one day, I just couldn't take it anymore. I did something very foolish. I took an overdose of aspirin to try and end it all." The more she confessed to Alan, the more ashamed she became. It was almost unbearable to continue! How utterly abhord he must be feeling now at the thought that he had almost married her, she told herself!

"I came too in hospital. My landlady had found me and telephoned for an ambulance. The doctors pumped my stomach and saved my life. Eventually, after a lot of cajoling, the ward sister persuaded me to give her my parent's phone number."

Alan held the lighter steady for her once more as she lit another cigarette, her hands trembling. He kept his silence as promised. "I was utterly terrified at the prospect of confronting my parents with the awful news that their only child was pregnant! How could I face them?" She took a long pull on her cigarette as she physically shook, reliving the ordeal.

"Mum and Dad were so sympathetic and gentle with me. I had fully expected to be scolded with recriminations. Instead, they both hugged and kissed me and told me that they loved me, and that we would work everything out. I'll never forget my dad. He sat down on the edge of my bed, tears rolling silently down his face. He kissed me on the cheek and told me hat no matter how desperate life seemed at times, to always remember that I had parents who loved me, and could turn to at any time."

She heaved a long sigh, and wiped the tears from her eyes. "I have never felt such remorse or guilt as I did then for the way I treated them, that is until now, my dearest," she hung her head, staring at the pebbles on the beach, not daring to look him in the eyes.

"My dearest darling Linda, you have nothing to feel guilty about, that was all a long time ago" he said, breaking his silence.

Once more she placed her finger on his lips, and tearfully looked into his eyes. "I am afraid that there is worse to come. Please hear me out, and then you will fully appreciate what a wicked person I am. I promise when you have heard me out you will fully appreciate why I can never marry you."

"I cannot believe that you have had much as a truly wicked thought in your entire life Linda Cartell! I dare say like all of us you have made your mistakes, but out of wickedness, never!" he said passionately.

"Alan, please. You promised." She implored "Please don't judge me until I have finished." She pulled on her cigarette nervously. He gave her hand a gentle squeezed and apologised.

"About two hours later, when my parents had gone to a hotel for the night, I began to feel very peculiar. I can only describe it as if I were being turned inside out. Then the pain struck! I screamed, a nurse came running to me, and that was the last thing I knew for ten whole days."

She sat in silence for a few seconds as she fought to control her tears. Regaining her composure, she braced herself, and plucked up the courage to continue.

"This is the most difficult and painful part, Alan, but I must tell you" she said in a whisper. "I was told that I had been rushed to the operating theatre, and the surgeon had delivered a baby boy. I had been in a coma since then until that moment."

Alan started to speak, but she interjected quickly. "Please let me continue, Alan, before my courage fails me" she pleaded. He complied as she appealed through tear filled eyes.

"I was ill for several weeks, and against my better instincts, I agreed very reluctantly to give my baby up for adoption, after great pressure from my parents to do so. I only saw him once, as I had been too ill to look after him, and the poor wee mite had been fighting for his own life in an incubator, I never saw him again."

"My poor, poor Linda, how you have suffered and tortured yourself needlessly, that was all in the past. How could you think that I would cancel our wedding? I love you. Do you understand? I love you!" he repeated with passion.

Tears flowed freely down Linda's cheeks. "Alan, being an unmarried mother is not the only reason I cannot marry you, my darling." She heaved a huge sigh, and stared at the pebbles at her feet.

She spoke very quietly, fighting to keep her tentative grip on her self control. "When I was released from hospital I returned to live with my parents. They were marvellous, and gradually, helped by their love and patience, I returned to health, and a reasonable frame of mind."

Once more, Alan held the cigarette lighter for her. "I returned to school and finished my final year. I do not know why it took so long, bit it was only after graduation that I realised that something was wrong. I had not had a menstruation period since leaving the hospital!"

Alan looked at there with a rather perplexed expression.

"When I told Mum, she broke down. She said that she had assumed that the surgeon had told me. She then had the unenviable task of telling her daughter that when my baby was delivered, they discovered I had suffered very serious internal damage, probably sustained at the hands of the baby's father when he beat me."

She smoked nervously, still staring at the pebble. "The surgeon had to perform a full hysterectomy to save my life. Now do you understand why I cannot marry you Alan? I cannot bear you a child, and I gave away the only child I had!" She broke down, weeping uncontrollably. She tried to pull away from him, but he tightened his grip on her.

"Darling. What terrible guilt you have endured. I love you Linda. I love you! Not for your child bearing capabilities! I am going to marry you, the woman I love!. He stated emphatically, brushing her hair from her tear stained cheeks. He kissed her tenderly. "Now tell me. Do you honestly think I would ever let you go?"

"My darling Alan, I do love you so! I have spent my life ridden by guilt. I know I was ill and under tremendous pressure from my parents, but I still gave up my child. I know they thought that they had my best interest at heart, but the guilt has never left me." She said, slowly regaining her composure.

"That settles the matter. Tomorrow, we are going home to Scotland and we are getting married as soon as possible. No argument." He held her in a tight embrace, and kissed her long and hard, their tongues intertwining in passionate bonding.

Linda was truly exhausted after her ordeal, and slept soundly on the homeward flight. She woke just a few minutes before touchdown, and was rather bleary eyed going through customs. The flight from Glasgow to the estate seemed more like a dream than reality.

A nice hot shower was sheer heaven on reaching Heather Cottage. She dimly remembered Alan's goodnight kiss when he brought her luggage into the house. A warm cup of hot chocolate, and then the heavenly delight of a soft caressing duvet! She slept for ten solid hours.

The familiar sound of her mother's voice greeted her when she awoke. She blinked her eyes in disbelief, feeling slightly disorientated.

"Hello sleepy head. Welcome back to the land of the living" her Mum said as she gave her a kiss.

"Mum. What on earth are you doing in Canada?" she blurted.

"You are not fully awake yet my dear. You are in Heather Cottage, silly. I arrived a few hours ago. I had to be the first to congratulate you!" her Mum replied, kissing and hugging her all at once

"Oh, mum. I was tired. I do apologise" she said.

"Now, you slip o n a robe and come through to the kitchen. I have breakfast ready, and you can tell me all about this fascinating man you are going to marry. I am thrilled for you, and intrigued at the same time" she smiled broadly at her daughter and began to hum "Here comes the bride" as she made her way to the kitchen.

"You gave me the most pleasant surprise when you phoned from Vancouver I am so happy for you dear. I simply had to come here as quickly as I could. I am so excited one would think he had proposed to me!" Mrs Cartell said, and they both laughed heartily.

"Thank you for coming, mum. I have missed you, you know. I am fully awake now" she said, and gave her Mum a nice hug.

"Now sit own and enjoy your bacon and eggs, and you can tell me all about my prospective son-in-law" her mum said hardly able to contain her curiosity.

Linda related her whole story, starting from when she first met Alan, through to that final traumatic night in Lions Bay."

"I am very proud of you Linda. You certainly held nothing back. That took great courage and fortitude. Alan obviously loves you very dearly. I know you will both be very happy. A marriage based on love and truth can only succeed. I am dying to meet him" her mother said as she poured more coffee.

"Well, now's your chance" Linda replied as she hear the familiar sound of the Range Rover approaching.

"How exciting!" Her mum said with undisguised delight.

Linda rushed to meet Alan as he drew up to the cottage. Greeting him with a long kiss, she took him in to introduce him to her mum.

"You have been holding out on me girl. You never said Alan is so handsome" her mum said with a broad grim as she was introduced to her soon to be son-in-law.

"I can see that you and I are going to get along famously, Mary, and of course it is patently obvious who Linda inherited her beauty from" Alan countered.

"Flattery will get you everywhere with me, I can see we are going to get along famously." Mary said rather mischieviously.

"Excuse me. I'll leave you two to enjoy your mutual admiration society, and pop into the bedroom and get dressed." Linda said. In the time it took her to shower and dress her mother and Alan were the best of friends.

"Hello dear. Alan and I were just discussing where you are going to live when you are married. He was telling me that the west wing of the mansion would seem the perfect space." Her Mum informed her gaily.

"You know more that I do mum. Alan and I haven't even discussed our domestic arrangements yet." Linda replied.

"Well, Alan was just saying that if you decide to go ahead with the alterations to the big house, the work could never be completed before the wedding, so I suggested that you stay here at the cottage."

"That is very kind of you Mum. But I would far rather discuss the matter with Alan before making any commitment. What do you think, Alan?" Linda asked her future husband already dreading what her mother may have persuaded him agreeing before he really realised what he had actually done!

"Linda. Someone has to be practical and look to more mundane matters. Do I detect a slight hint of pique in your voice?" Her mother queried.

"Not really. It's just that you are not here five minutes and you already are giving me the impression that you want to try and influence our decision making. I know that sounds harsh to you Alan, but my mother could coax state secrets from the head of M.I.5. without his being aware of it, and probably having agreed to lend her the crown jewels for the next party as well!"

"Linda. I am the one who volunteered the information to your Mum. Now if you are up tight with anyone, it should be me." Alan said, "Don't you think you owe your mum an apology?"

"Alan, you'll get used to our little ways. Linda and I enjoy our…..let's call debates. We are not arguing. Honestly. It is a mother/daughter thing. We do tend to say things that probably sound dreadful to others, but we both know that they are said in the spirit of love and respect for each other. You'll get used to our vociferous points of view in time. Believe me." Mary promised.

"Honestly, darling. I would never say anything to deliberately hurt Mum, nor would she ever hurt me." Linda assured him.

Alan accepted a cup of coffee from Mary and shook his head."Women! I'll never understand them!" he said, looking very perplexed.

Chapter Ten

The next few days were spent organising the wedding arrangements. Alan and Linda both wished for a quiet church ceremony, followed by a reception at the local hotel they had launched at on the fateful day they had gone to Glasgow.

Alan had taken great delight in showing both Linda and Mary the mansion house. They were both stunned by its sheer size! The house was a grand old Georgian mansion, granite built. The fifty six rooms it boasted had been modified over the years to accommodate offices and the staff dining room and kitchen, a lounge and a games room. The upper floors were converted into flats for personnel who lived on site, which most of them did. A few married ones preferred to live in the local village.

Alan enjoyed relating to Mary tales of when he was young, describing in detail the parties and the grand balls his parents used to hold and how he and his brother used to sneak out of bed to watch the festivities. "In those days of course Mary my father was held in awe by the locals. They were no different to others of their ilk, I suspect, they honestly believed that they were superior to the working classes, a trait I am afraid my father took to the grave. Even though financially he was good as bankrupt, he felt that it was his right that the bank should extend him unlimited credit! He just never got to grips with modern life, I am sorry to say. Ahh, well, it is all in the past, and at least I still have the estate."

Linda was very quiet on the return to the cottage, hardly noticing the beautiful sunset.

"A penny for them" Alan said.

"Pardon?" she replied absentmindedly.

"I said a penny for your thoughts. You have been miles away, darling."

"I am sorry, Alan. I was thinking about the house. You obviously have invested a lot of time and money building the offices and flats. I think it would be very unfair, selfish even, to start changing everything, and especially uprooting the people who live in it. Couldn't we just live in Heather Cottage?" Linda replied.

"I agree entirely with your reasoning, dear, with one tiny wee exception" he said. "Heather Cottage belongs to your mum. I know you have offered us its use for the duration Mary, but I feel that we really must have our own house, so I propose that instead of altering the mansion, we simply build from scratch."

"If you would rather do that, I am more than willing, it would be a unique experience to build my own home from scratch." Linda answered, feeling rather excited about the prospect!

"Right, that settles the matter." Alan said, and immediately performed a u-turn, taking both Linda and her mum by surprise. "I think we have enough daylight left." Alan said as he headed past the mansion, and then took a small track which went off to the left. A few minutes later, they emerged from the large stand of conifers they had been driving through into a clearing which afforded the most glorious view of the mountains and the loch.

"This is simply stunning! The view from here is a s good as the view the house at Lions Bay has in Canada!" Linda enthused.

"I can only say that it is breath taking. What a marvellous setting to build a house on!" Mary said, "You would be the envy of everyone I know if you had a house here Linda."

"Isn't it spectacular! I can just imagine a house like the one referred to in Canada Mum. I t is absolutely beautiful. You would love it." Her daughter answered.

"Mary is more than welcome to visit Lions Bay any time Linda, after all, the house is mine. Well, that is to say, ours, actually." Alan explained to her.

"Do you mean that you own the house there, I thought that it was rented for the duration of the negotiations. I never dreamt that you owned it!" Linda said in surprise.

"I thought you realised it was mine. I bought it, or rather I built it a couple of years ago. I t is very handy when I have to go to Canada, which is quite often during the course of the year. As a matter of fact the architect who designed it is coming here tomorrow. I phoned him to design the alterations for the big house, but he can design a house for us instead." Alan said nonchalantly.

"That sounds wonderful, Alan. Perhaps he could do something similar to the one in Canada. I simply adored it." Linda said hopefully.

"This house is to be our home darling, and anything, any ides you may have, shall be incorporated in the plans. Anything you have ever wanted in a home, now is your chance to realise. Write down al your thoughts, and Jim Mckay, he's the architect, by the way, will be only too pleased to carry out your instructions if at all feasible. I assure you. You'll like him, he is a great guy."

"I am sure that we will get along just fine. If he designed the house at Lions Bay, I cannot fail but like him." Linda replied with warmth, and delivered a kiss on the cheek to Alan. "I love you" she whispered.

As they were entering the Range Rover once more, Linda suddenly stopped and looked at Alan rather sheepishly and said "would it be going overboard if I asked Jim to design a Jacuzzi inside the house. I have always dreamed of one?"

"My darling, you can have ten Jacuzzi's if your heart desires them. Don't be afraid to ask for anything. Remember, expense is not a consideration. This is to be our home, as I said, therefore now is the time to try and think of how you would like it to look, not only in the structural design, but think seriously about the interior as well. I'll arrange to have an interior designer to be flown here tomorrow, and you can bounce ideas off each other. I am positive that the end of result will be to yours and my satisfaction." He started as the car negotiated the track back to the road. "I'll have to remember to contact the builders in the morning that I'll need this track built into a proper road as soon as possible too." He added. "You are very quiet, Mary. I almost forgot you were here."

"I have no doubt that you will have some invaluable ideas yourself. You are the ideal person to make sure your daughter does not skimp on anything. Remember, money is no object, and I am relying on you to encourage her to demand only the best of everything and of everyone." He said to his awestruck future mother-in-law.

"It will take me a little while to get used to the notion that money isn't a consideration, Alan." Mary answered honestly, "but I am sure that I can adjust to the idea rather quickly" she added!

"That is what I want to hear. Positive thinking!" he replied, and gave Mary a peck on the cheek!

The Range Rover was approaching the cottage when Linda suddenly said, "I have been meaning to ask you Alan, why did you sell Dad Heather Cottage? You certainly could not have been needing the money!"

"Have you never told Linda the story Mary?" He asked of her.

"I am afraid that I don't know the circumstances, Alan. He never went into details, and I was not curious really. I always left business matters to Arthur." She explained.

"It is a long story, ladies. I'll explain over a nice coffee and hopefully a scone or two?"

The gathered in the lounge armed with a pot of coffee and a plate piled high with scones Jeannie Campbell had very kindly dropped into them that morning.

"Well, curiosity is getting the better of us both. Just why did you sell my Dad the cottage?"

"As you know, your Dad was in the RAF in fact he was in the same squadron as my father. They were pals from the moment they met, and remained so for life, actually."

"So it was your father Arthur used to come to Scotland to fish with!" Mary interjected "I never realised that. He always wanted me to come, but I had no notion of going fishing, I am afraid" she added.

"I am astounded he never mentioned it. According to father, Arthur was quite a character, full of life with a marvellous sense of humour. Rather heroic too, as you no doubt know."

"Are you sure you are talking about the right man Alan?" Linda queried. "Dad never spoke about the war days. I have always assumed that he had a nice quiet time behind some desk."

"Arthur didn't like to speak about his experiences. He was a prisoner of war for almost two years, dear, but he just said that it was not too bad, could have been worse." He Mum said. "He did get presented with a medal, I knew that much, but he simply put it in the drawer and forgot it, I guess. His only reference to the war was that it was best forgotten, and he took his own advice I suppose, because he never mentioned those days really, no even to me."

"The medal he was awarded was the Distinguished Flying Cross, and he didn't get that for peeling spuds, I can assure you" Alan said. "He certainly was an extremely modest fellow. You have to admire him."

"Do you know what he did to be decorated? I am totally astounded! I always thought I knew dad very well. It looks though that I knew precious little in fact." Linda said a little saddened.

"I don't know the details, I only know that he more or less sacrificed his own fighter to save others, resulting in his being shot down over France. He ended up in the same P.O.W. camp as my father, he was shot down three days previously. I do know that they escaped several times together, always being recaptured, unfortunately. The Germans got a bit fed up with their exploits, and transferred them to Colditz. They were there for the duration of the war. That is basically all I know, ladies." Alan refilled his cup, and helped himself to another scone.

"This is more incredulous than a novel. Here I am being told about my father's war feats from the man I love, who turns out to be the son of his best friend! No one would believe it if it was used for a plot for a story! Incredulous! Linda said again.

"I suppose it is rather strange when you think on it" Alan replied. "Obviously must be the fickle hand of fate" he concluded.

"The only time I ever heard Arthur mention the war was when the TV series about Colditz was on. He said to me once, "It wasn't all bad". That was all he said." Mary told them. "I knew that Arthur's Air Force pal was a Scotsman named Ferguson, but I never really associated him with you Alan. I am astonished, life is funny at times."

"Yes, I guess it must be remarkable for you both. Arthur was obviously a modest man. Some men are. My father was the opposite, he was like an open book. He was overly fond of the whisky, and loved to reminisce about his war years. I don't really the full story, but I do know that Arthur saved my dad's life on at least one of their escapes, and my dad never forgot" Alan said thoughtfully.

"Father was not only a friend of Arthur's, it went beyond that. He never exactly said why, only that Arthur saved his life on more than one occasion during their incarceration. He always wanted to give your Dad something to repay him in some small way, which your dad would not hear of! One year when he was up on a fishing holiday, he saw Heather Cottage, and fell in love with it. He asked father if it was for sale."

Alan paused to take a sip of coffee. "Father was all set to give the cottage to Arthur as a gift, when his solicitor reminded him of the terms of my grandfather's will. To let you understand, father was a follower of the Sport of Kings, as he always referred to his addiction with gambling on horses. He was to put it kindly, a disaster area when it came to judging horseflesh. He lost a fortune in his lifetime. His love of racing did not escape his father's attention, and he willed the estate in such a way my father could never sell it in whole or in part. Grandfather's way of protecting the inheritance for future generations, I assume"

"Does that mean that you cannot sell the estate either?" Mary inquired.

"That is correct, Mary. I am tied by the will also. Try as he did with all his energy and a great deal of expense to find a loophole, father had to admit defeat in the end and tell his friend that it was impossible to sell or even gift him the cottage. However, about three years ago, I ran into Arthur in London. We had lunch together, and the terms of the will came up in conversation. Arthur was always sorry that my father had been frustrated by the conditions laid down by my grandfather. Arthur never fully realised the extent to which his friends gambling extended. Father kept the side of his life from him. However, I started thinking about father's wish that Arthur could have the cottage, and I set a team of solicitors to work to try and resolve the problem. Three months later, I was delighted to contact your Dad to inform him that there was indeed a loophole, and that father's wishes were to be fulfilled." Alan smiled with satisfaction.

"After a lot research, it was discovered that under Scots Law, it was possible to sell Arthur the raw materials that the structure is actually built of, as long as the said property has been vacant for more than on year. The land the materials were sited on could be leased to the buyer for any length of time. I duly sold your dad the stones and slates for the grand sum of one penny, and leased the land to him for one pound per year for one hundred years. All perfectly legal! I think father would have approved." He said with a little pride.

"You are amazing, Alan Ferguson." Linda said, stunned by the whole story.

"I am sure that your father would have been very proud of you." Mary said, and kissed his cheek tenderly. "I know that I could never wish for a finer son-in-law!"

Alan suddenly started to laugh. "I wish you would inform the press that I am an angel at heart, and not really an ugly capitalist. Well certainly not an ugly capitalist, perhaps just an ugly angel!" he quipped.

"Alan Ferguson! You are the limit. Can't you be serious for two whole minutes at a time?" Linda said, laughing as she spoke.

Chapter Eleven

David Eaton was very surprised that morning when Mr Selwyn had sent for him. What on earth could he want with him? David had only been with the company for eight months, his first full time job since graduation. His B.A. in business management had been hard earned at Exeter University, and now the managing director, no less, had sent for him! The company employed in excess of nine hundred people, and he was a very lowly dogsbody really at the bottom of the management tree. He could not figure for the life of him what Mr Selwyn wanted with him!

He frantically combed his memory to see if he could recall making some gigantic error which could lead to his dismissal. He quickly pushed this aside. Reason told him that if he had indeed done something catastrophic, or even if he were to be made redundant, it would surely be his immediate superior, who would be delegated the unpleasant task of telling him, most certainly not the managing director!

Promotion? The same answer, Simpson, his supervisor, would inform him. He was at a complete loss, undoubtedly when he did reach Mr Selwyn's office on the tenth floor, it would turn out to be a practical joke!

That was it! A practical joke! Of course! Why on earth hadn't he twigged to it before now? Well, he'd show them, he would play along to the end! He would go to Selwyn's office. He knew now that there was little doubt that the Managing director's private secretary would throw him out on his ear!

One thing was for sure, the female who had actually phoned him at his desk to inform him that he was to present himself before the great man at eleven a.m. prompt was very convincing!

Being cautious by instinct, he had called Mr Selwyn's office that he was indeed the David Eaton in question, and much to his surprise the voice on the other end of the line had confirmed so. Now of course he was certain that someone must have interfered with his desk phone to divert his call. The girl had to be in on the joke as well. But who was she? The only puzzle was who would play such a prank, and why pick on him?

The moment of truth was nigh, he mused as he reached the tenth floor. He stood momentarily outside the office door, nervously straightening his tie. Taking his courage in both hands, he knocked and entered.

He was greeted by a very attractive brunette, elegantly attired in a pastel grey two piece lambswool suit. She greeted him with a smile, showing her perfect white teeth. The desk nameplate bore the title of Mrs M. Martin.

"Good morning, Mr Eaton?"

David was dumbfounded! The voice was the voice on the telephone, and she was expecting him! "Ye Y Yes" he stammered.

"Please take a seat" she said in a friendly tone, as she picked up her in-house phone and informed her boss that his eleven a.m. appointment had arrived. "Please go through, Mr Selwyn is expecting you" she said as she replaced the receiver.

A very nervous and very perplexed young man rose from his chair and made his way in rather a daze to the large mahogany door with the gleaming brass plate engraved in Old English lettering, Managing Director.

"Come in" a deep male voice said in answer to David's knock. He entered the inner sanctum as in a dream, fully expecting to wake with a start at any second.

A large rotund man in his early sixties sat behind an enormous desk with a shiny glass top, on which sat no fewer than five phones and a computer console. He smiled and stood, proffering his hand as David entered.

"Nice to meet you David. I am sorry it has taken so long to make your acquaintance, but what with the pressure of business and all that you know, you understand?" He smiled, making David more nervous than ever. "I normally try and have at least one informal get together with new junior management, but this has been an exceptional period…" This was a deliberate lie told to impress the gentleman seated on the large sofa on the far side of the room, who David only now noticed.

"Ahh. This is Mr Gray from head office" Selwyn said by way of introduction. David thought that he hadn't heard correctly as he shook hands with this tall man who looked vaguely familiar. Did Selwyn say that Mr Gray was from head office? He must have misconstrued what Selwyn had said. This was the head office of South Software Ltd.

"Please take a seat David. You may smoke if you wish" Mr Gary said in a friendly manner as he gestured David to the sofa.

"I don't smoke, thank you sir" He replied.

"Very wise" Gray said to him, nodding his head in agreement.

"You are undoubtedly curious to why you are here, David?" Selwyn began, "As you are probably aware, South Software is a division in the Alan Arnold Group of companies, of which Mr Gray is deputy chairman. W are an extremely progressive company, to say the least. When an individual shows drive and promise, the word is relayed to head office. This has happened in your case, I am pleased to tell you David. I think Mr Gray shall take over from this point." Selwyn smiled at David, who wasn't really listening fully to what Selwyn was saying. Now he knew why Gray seemed familiar. He had seen him on TV many times on the news!

"Thank you Mr Selwyn" Gray said. "I am sure that neither David nor I will object to you keeping your luncheon engagement." He smiled, but is eyes remained cold.

Selwyn flushed visibly. But stood and shook hands with them, and then excused himself and left the office. David had seen raw power being portrayed in the movies, but this was the first time he had witnessed it being used in real life, a truly awe inspiring experience, yet accomplished with great aplomb. Young David was tremendously impressed, but now utterly bewildered as to why he was there!

"You seemed rather surprised to hear that Southern Software is a division of Alan Arnold Group, David." Mr Gray observed.

"Well, yes actually. I didn't know that. Was I so obvious? I thought Southern was an independent company. I mean, after all. I have been here eight months and I have never heard Alan Arnold Group mentioned once, or a head office for that matter." David defended.

"A reflection of the efficiency Southern software operates. Head office intercedes in the daily operations of a company only if the need arises due to an internal problem, otherwise the management is left to manage, and that it as it should be." Mr Gray answered.

"However, I have no doubt that you will grasp, and appreciate our philosophy on the requirements of any business we take a serious look at with the intent of buying. If it does not meet with our criteria as to its day to day management, then we quickly lose interest. There have been a few exceptions to the rule, of course, but very few indeed. However, I digress from the subject. You are no doubt wondering why you are actually here?"

"Well, more than a little, to tell you the truth." David replied.

"Naturally. Well, I'll explain as briefly as I possibly can. You have been singled out as someone with the potential we look for in our junior management programme. Your immediate supervisor, Mr Simpson has reported that you are full of ideas, and we are always looking for ways to improve the efficiency of your department, and more than one suggestion where you think the company as a whole can be improved. We like to encourage free thinking within the group, and that is the reason I am here, David.

David flushed bright red. "I have made a few suggestions, but Mr Simpson shot them down in flames, on financial grounds usually. Are you quite certain you have the right person sir? I hardly think I merit special attention based upon my success rate regarding any of my ideas being implemented." He answered truthfully.

"David, You are the correct man I came to see. Mr Simpson was basing his evaluations within the combines of this one company. Fortunately he passed on your suggestions to a higher level at head office. We take an overall view of the group, rather than a parochial one. Your ideas met with same favour. I am here to offer you a promotion to a special group in head office David. A very special section. A sort of think tank. We are sure that you have the special type of flair that is required." Mr Gray said with sincerity.

David was flabbergasted. He was being invited to join the company elite, he knew that much for sure!

"I realise that this is very sudden, and without doubt a tremendous opportunity, David. Before you leap, let me explain a few things regarding the section you are being invited to join. The drawbacks first. The think tank is located in Scotland. The highlands of Scotland, to be exact. The wilderness would be an apt description, I think it's fair to say. You would be based on the estate, living and working in the mansion house. Are you still interested?" Gary asked

"Is the estate very remote?"

"Got it in one. Very remote. This is the major consideration David. We try to provide a package to alleviate the boredom and loneliness that everyone experiences from time to time. It is inevitable, I am afraid. We are all human. People raised in an urban environment suffer depression when isolated in the country for any length of time has been our experience" He paused to light a cigarette, offering David one.

"I don't smoke, thank you" he said.

"Good on you, a nasty habit. The accommodation in the house is first class, as is the cuisine on offer twenty four hours a day. Living in is all found, so your salary is subject to income tax only, leaving the bulk of your earnings intact. This is one benefit most people appreciate. The other major drawback is of course you are enquired to live in seven days a week, due to the remoteness. To compensate for this, members of the head office team employed at the estate, enjoy a few perks, I guess you could say. To compensate for the enforced remoteness we work a rota of six weeks on and fourteen days off. We also provide free flights to your home or to any part of the world the company has hotels. Free accommodation is provided in any hotel that has a vacancy at the required time. We operate hotels in fifty six countries, so the choice is wide and varied. The staff seem to approve of the system, we have had no complaints, or even a transfer request to return to civilisation, so to speak." Bret Gray said with a trace of a smile on his lips.

David sat absolutely awe struck. "I have to repeat myself sir. But are you absolutely sure you have the right David Eaton?"

Bret Gray laughed and nodded his head. "I am absolutely certain David. I'll give you a week to decide."

"I have already decided sir. I'll take the job. No qualms." David replied with enthusiasm.

"I am delighted to hear it. Welcome to the team David. You are now a member of the think tank, and there will be no more of the "sir", we are very informal at head office. The name is Bret"

"Yes sir...sorry Bret," David replied, feeling slightly awkward at calling the deputy chairman of the Alan Arnold Group by his first name.

"Something I forgot to mention. You would have remembered when I was away no doubt. Your salary. Thirty five thousand pounds a year to start. Is that alright?"

"Yes. Terrific. Thank you" came the numbed reply. That was more than twice his current earnings!

"That settles that then. How about a spot of lunch?" Bret asked, taking David once again by complete surprise.

"Yes thanks. There is a nice restaurant across the road." David suggested.

"I think that will do admirably. Lead on." Bret answered.

"I believe you live alone" Bret said as they settled at their table.

"Yes. Mum died four months ago. Dad was killed out in South Africa nine years ago, it must be." His eyes filled, and he valiantly fought back the tears. "Mum fought breast cancer for about two years, but it got her in the end, to be truthful, it was probably a blessing in disguise." He reflected.

"I am sorry, David. Your Mum's passing must be very painful for you, "Bret said sympathetically.

"Thank you. I guess it will hurt for a time. But people tell me that time is the great healer. I am not so sure. Mum and Dad were not my natural parents, actually. I was adopted at birth. But they were real parents to me, probably more than my real parents would have been. I loved them both dearly." He said emotionally.

"I am sure they kneww that David. And I am equally sure that their presence will always be with you."

"Thank you, sir. Sorry, I mean Bret. That is the most comforting thought I have heard since Mum passed away. You are a very wise person and I am grateful." David replied. A sense of weight being lifted from his shoulders filled him with relief, and he relaxed completely.

"Not at all, David. I just understand what you have been going through. I was slightly younger than you when my own mother died. My father was killed in the war when I was only a toddler, so I have no memories of him. I was raised by my mother, and I know that she is still with me, thirty odd years after her death. I don't think it is imagination. That kind of love really dies." Bret told him. He lit a cigarette, giving himself a few precious seconds to regain his composure.

"Do you live in a house or a flat?" He asked David.

"A house actually. Mum left me the bungalow in her will."

"Mmm. I see, may I suggest that you rent your house for say, a year? You would be wise not to sell at this stage. After all, you may not settle to the life in the highlands."

"I would never dream of selling Mum's house." David replied. "I don't even know if I could bear renting it to a stranger."

"I know it is a difficult time. May I suggest that you let the company arrange renting the bungalow for you? I can guarantee that only the highest calibre of person would be considered. We are the largest property company in the country, and I give you my word that everything will be done correctly and professionally. You will have enough on your plate settling in to you new position without any added burden."

"Your right, of course. I have your word?" Bret nodded, taking no offence that his word could be called into question. "I would be grateful if you would arrange things for me." David said.

"Consider it as good as done! Now, you are to discuss this move with no one at Southern. I will inform Mr Selwyn of your transfer. You go to your desk and collect your personal things, and leave the office. I know it sounds a bit cloak and dagger, but we keep the think tank rather hush hush. Any problem with that?" Bret asked,

"No. No problem at all. Other people might wonder where I have gone, though." He replied.

"That is the natural reaction. Mr Selwyn can take care of that matter, Not your problem. Now I suggest that you go home and start packing." Bret smiled, then added, "You can tell them that you have been transferred to head office, just don't mention the think tank. On reflection, it is perhaps more prudent to inform your colleagues yourself of your transfer."

"I think that is the best suggestion too. When will I actually have to leave for Scotland?" David asked, excitement beginning to build.

"Do you think you can be ready in two days?"

"Well. I am sure that I can be ready in two day, but I am not sure if I can arrange to have the gas and electric read and terminated in that time scale" he replied, his brain beginning to work again after the shocks it had sustained that morning.

"Don't worry about the services or council taxes etcetera, the company will take care of all that. You just be packed and ready to go in two days, please."

"I'll be ready. No sweat." David replied in the vernacular.

"Good. My secretary will contact you tomorrow with the details of your travel arrangements. It has been a pleasure meeting you, David, and I know that we'll be seeing a lot of each other in the future. I am looking forward to it." Bret shook hands, and then departed to meet with Mr Selwyn.

Later in the afternoon, Bret Gray boarded the company executive jet at Heathrow airport, and settled in his seat as the pilot smoothly lifted the plane into the air, bound for Glasgow. An hour and a quarter later he was on board the twin engine Piper aircraft heading for the estate, and an appointment with Alan Ferguson.

A car met him at the runaway and sped him to the mansion. He arrived exactly two hours and five minutes after take of from Heathrow. "Hi Alan. Good to see you." Bret said as he was met at the door by his friend.

"Hi, Bret. What is all the mystery? Have you discovered gold?" Alan said feeling in very good humour. The architect had arrived and the plans for the new house were going ahead leaps and bounds. Very satisfying indeed for everyone.

Bret looked at Alan for a moment before answering.

"I have some news for you, old boy. I have found him."

Alan looked at Bret in disbelief. "Did I hear you right? Did you say that you have found him?!"

"That is what I said. It has taken the services of the worlds best detective agency. But they tracked him eventually. The records were destroyed in a fire at the town hall shortly after his birth. That is why it was so difficult. You'll never guess where he was? Right under our noses. He works for us, would you believe?!"

"What ?!!" Alan said in sheer amazement.

"I kid you not, Alan. He actually works for us! Would you also believe that he was earmarked to be offered a position up here with the think tank! I couldn't believe it when all the pieces fell together." Bret said, smiling form ear to ear.

"Have you spoken to him yet, Bret?"

"Yes. I was with him this morning. He arrives here in two days time. I have told him nothing, of course. He has no inkling of who you are, or of your connection with Linda. I do know that he has no inkling of who his birth mother is, he has tried to trace her, without success. That is entirely your prerogative as to whether you tell him and Linda. His name is David. David Eaton. I have done my bit, the rest is up to you, now, old friend. I honestly wish you luck. I would not want to be in your shoes for all the tea in China. I don't envy you one little bit. I hope you know what you are doing, Alan."

"So do I Bret. So do I" came the reply in a hoarse whisper.

Chapter Twelve

Linda was sitting in the living room of the cottage enjoying a cup of coffee, listening to her mum with great interest, ever since Alan had imparted what little he knew about her father's war exploits and his lifelong friendship with Alan's father, her mum had gradually given her an insight into the man, the very private man, whom she thought she knew everything that was worth knowing about, she was slowly realising she actually knew very little about him in actual fact!

All children take their parents for granted, don't they? She reckoned that she was no different from most offspring in thinking that her Dad was just an ordinary man, dull, and dare she say, boring even? After all, he led an ordinary boring existence like most people do. How was she to know that he was a war hero if no one told her? She naturally had assumed that he had a dull boring office job during the war in keeping with his peacetime occupation.

How wrong! Arthur Cartell, her own father that she had always taken for granted, and regarded as quite unadventurous, and if she was really truthful, thought him an old fuddy duddy, had achieved more, and probably done more by the time he was twenty one, than she could ever hope to If she lived for ten life times!

Time had flown with astonishing speed. When they had returned from Canada it seemed then that the wedding day was far off in the future, ample time to do everything that had to be done. Now suddenly, it was only three days, a mere seventy one and a half hours away, to be precise!

Both her Mum and Jeannie Campbell had been wonderful. Goodness only knows what she would have done without them. She mentally went over the arrangements once again in her mind for their "very quiet" wedding, as Alan referred to it. Very quiet indeed! The guest list had escalated from fewer than twenty, to over one hundred and sixty, no less!

After giving the matter careful consideration, Alan had produced a list of one hundred and thirty-two he insisted were essential to be invited, or they would never forgive him. And men have the brass neck to talk bout women being fickle her mum and Jeannie had both said, voicing her own thoughts perfectly!

The wedding service was being conducted in the local village church. The reception was to have been held in the hotel, but due to the guest list swelling some what, it was now necessary to hold it in the ball room of the mansion, which had been used as the dining and recreational facility for the staff for several years now. Surprisingly, no one complained at the temporary loss of this facility, much to Linda's surprise. Alan simply said that the staff were delighted for them, and the room would return to normal use after the wedding. No sweat, was the term they used, he told her.

Linda had gone down to London for a couple of days previously with her Mum and Jeannie, who was utterly thrilled, to help her choose her outfit. Eventually, she settled on a pastel pink cashmere woollen suit, with a full pleated skirt. The most beautiful Japanese silk blouse with two delicately embroidered turtledoves across the bust, they were all agreed that this was the most beautiful blouse any of them had ever seen. She indulged herself with the most expensive silk lingerie that Harrods supply, pure silk hosiery, and beautiful calf skin two and a half inch high heeled shoes to match her suit. The ensemble was completed with a wide brimmed silk and chiffon hat, which the millinery department had specially made her within a twenty four hour period!

The flowers were on order locally, pink orchids and white roses, her Dad's favourite flowers. The only slightly annoying thing was that when she went to pay the bill at Harrods, no less, the bill was on the house! They naturally had learned that Miss Cartell was marrying no less a figure than Alan Ferguson!

"That was very kind of them, my dear." Alan had said when she told him. "You are going to have to get used to things like this happening from time to time, I am afraid. The funny thing about this life is that when you desperately need money, usually no one wants to give it to you, and when you don't need it, no one wants to take the damned stuff from you! Ironic really!"

David Eaton had settled in very well. Everyone had made him welcome, and he felt thoroughly relaxed and at home in the big house. Bret was correct when he had told him that they didn't go in for formality. Everybody was on first name basis only, to his amazement. He soon realised that this led to a relaxed attitude, very pleasant working conditions, and the friendliest atmosphere he had ever encountered. He totally loved it!

Even Alan Ferguson, the chairman of the group, insisted on being called by his first name! The chairman, no less!

David had been enlightened as to who Alan really was on his first day. He was to say the least, astonished by the story, but on reflection, it was no more astonishing than the place itself!

Ideas and theories abounded, and no mater how bizarre, or mundane even, each was afforded equal consideration. David revelled in the free and easy attitude that permeated throughout the entire work place. So much so, that one tended to forget that it was a work place! He felt very privileged to be part of the team. He smiled as he reflected that he did feel part of the team in such a short space of time.

Alan played a waiting game, deciding that he right moment would present itself, rather than going in with both feet and telling David certain facts that he might be the happiest person on earth to hear, or could completely backfire and lead to catastrophe! He was in a very delicate position, albeit of his own making, and he had to handle the situation properly, with tact and diplomacy. There would be no second chances! He was gambling not only with young David's future, but also taking a dangerous gamble with his own relationship with Linda. Would she understand if things went wrong? He knew that she could be deeply hurt, and he was taking the calculated risk that what he was contemplating was the correct course to follow.

He had spent sleepless nights pondering the quandary, but great as the risks were, the even greater rewards to be gained if everything worked out proved the determining factor. He had to play his hand, win or lose! He had always trusted his instincts in business, and he must trust them now. This was probably the most important decision he had ever made in his entire life, and he had steeled his nerve to see it through!

The following morning, Mrs Cartell decided to take a walk along the shore of the loch, and enjoy the fresh crisp air. The sun was shining, and she was enjoying the break from the last minute checking and rechecking of endless details pertaining to the wedding. The immense amount of detail a wedding demanded always astonished her, and, thrilled as she was for her daughter, she for one would sigh a sigh of relief when it was all over!

Stopping to admire the sun's reflection on the waters of the loch, she became aware of a young man sitting on a rock a little distance along the shore from her. He seemed very deep in thought, and totally oblivious to her presence.

Deciding it would be unkind to disturb his thoughts, she opted to retrace her steps and return to the cottage and have a nice cup of tea, glancing in the young man's direction as she left. This time she took a closer look at him, and stood transfixed to the spot, letting out an involuntary squeal. For a moment, she thought she was seeing a ghost!

David looked up when he heard the gasp, and was astonished to see a lady standing a short distance from him, her hand cupped to her mouth, staring rather dazedly at him.

"I am sorry, I didn't mean to startle you" he said.

"No. I am the one who should be apologising. I startled you. You must think me a silly woman. But at first sight you reminded me of someone. I honestly thought that I was seeing a ghost! "Mary Cartell answered, feeling very embarrassed by the whole episode.

"I can assure you that I am no ghost, but the way I am feeling, I would probably welcome it if I was at this moment in time" he said very despondently.

"Oh, don't say a thing like that on such a beautiful morning. I am sure that whatever is troubling you can't be that bad, surely?" Mrs Cartell replied sympathetically.

"Right at this minute it seems so, I am afraid. But please don't be alarmed. I am not contemplating suicide or anything foolish like that." David said hastily.

"Thank goodness for that, you gave me quite a start. Listen. My cottage is only a short walk from here. Why don't you come and have a nice cup of tea? There is no one at home at the moment, and to tell you the truth, I could use a bit of company myself. Especially that of such a handsome young man!" she quipped, hoping he would respond.

David studied this elegant and very persuasive lady, and he just had to relent and agree to accompany her to her cottage and have a cup of tea! He was feeling very low in spirits, and to say the least, extremely confused. He couldn't understand why, but somehow this perfect stranger had a calming effect, indeed a reassuring effect on him. She exuded great inner strength which he could literally feel. He had never experienced this before, and it mystified him. Strangest of all, they had only just met, he didn't know her name, and yet he felt as though he had known her all his life!

"You win. I'll come for a cup of tea" he said, trying valiantly to smile. "I am David Eaton" he added.

"Mary Cartell. I am pleased to meet you David; she replied, smiling charmingly.

"I am sorry if I startled you, Mrs Cartell, I really didn't mean to"

"Not at all, my dear boy, but if we are going to be friends, and I certainly hope that we are, you just call me Mary" she countered as they shook hands.

"Mary it is. You know, I feel we are friends already." David said, smiling this time voluntarily. "Have you lived here long, Mary?" he asked.

"I don't actually live here. I live in London. I have a cottage here, and I visit as often as I can. I do love it here."

They continued chatting as they made their way to the cottage, strolling at a leisurely pace. Mary made the promised cup of tea when they finally arrived, which she served along with home made pancakes and home made strawberry jam Jeannie Campbell had made earlier.

The hot liquid relaxed David. Mary chatted away in a soft soothing voice, easing the turmoil that enveloped him. He did like this very nice lady who had befriended him. She was like the friendly grandmother in a children's fairytale, he mused.

Mary could see that the young man was wrestling with a great problem, and she used all her guile and charm to help him relax and to talk about what was troubling him. He was extremely reticent at first, and Mary chatted away gaily with small talk. She had a life time of experience.

Imperceptibly, her strategy worked, and David found himself pouring his heart out to her. He told of his adoption as a baby, and of his adoptive parents. How the family had moved to South Africa when he was quite young, and of his life in Durban.

His dad died when he was only fourteen and financial circumstances had been forced his mother to return to England with her son. David had hated England, the weather and his school when he first arrived back, but slowly he adjusted to his new circumstances, and gradually grew to like the place, much to his own surprise.

Completing High School, he had gone on to University, achieving a Master of Arts in Business studies. During his last ear at University his mother had become ill, and unfortunately she died shortly after he graduated. He had just started work a short time, and she was so proud of him, when she was taken form him, he related tearfully.

Having been fortunate enough to have secured employment with Southern Software he had fortunately no financial problems after her death, just a great sense of loss, and loneliness, which still haunted him.

He then told of his interview and subsequent transfer, and how well he liked his new position, and his new colleagues. He loved living on the estate, and found the silence to be to his liking, much to his surprise. He had never lived in the country before, and he told Mary how nervous he had been about coming. Even although he had been warned by Bret Gray that the estate was very remote, he had never imagined it to be so remote. He never knew that anywhere so remote actually existed in Britain, but now he was here, he admitted to Mary that he loved it!

"Unfortunately, there always has to be a downside" he said with a large sigh.

"What do you mean, a downside, David?" Mary queried.

"I'll try and explain. I was asked to accompany Alan Ferguson on a fishing trip last night. I was told that he did this with new chaps to get acquainted. Do you know Alan Ferguson?" he asked her.

"Yes. I know, Alan. He strikes me as a perfect gentleman, David. Surely he is not the one responsible for your grief this morning?" Mary said with concern.

"I thought, like you, that he was a perfect gentleman, too. I am not so sure now." He answered.

"Why? What on earth could Alan have done to upset you so?" She was intrigued, but almost afraid to hear the answer, even more afraid that she already knew it!

"Well, we went on the loch in a small motor boat. He asked me if I had fished before, and when I told him I hadn't, he baited my hook, and taught me how to cast. We chatted about how I was settling in. Was I enjoying the work, and things like that. Then somehow, I really don't know how, I found myself telling Alan about my adoption, and my whole life up to the present. I still don't know how the subject came about, or who raised it even.

I guess it must have been me. He paused to add milk to the fresh cup of tea that Mary had just poured.

"Alan then asked me the strangest question, which rather took me aback, to say the least." David continued.

"He asked if I had ever given any thought as to who my natural mother was, and if I had ever tried to trace her." Mary sat in silence, too afraid now to say anything.

"I really didn't know what to say at first. After all it was a very personal question, and quite frankly, none of his business. He just sat in the boat in silence, toying with his fishing rod, waiting for me to reply. I suddenly felt very foolish, and I told him that I had. Probably in common with all adoptees, wondered from time to time who my natural mother was, and what she looked like, and if I perhaps looked like her. I had tried only recently to trace my parents, but with no success. Alan just nodded."

David sipped his tea and gave a slight shrug. I told him that with mum passing away, it didn't seem fair, and I know it is irrational, but I wanted to find my natural mother, not out of sentiment, but If I was honest, to vent my pent up anger on her for being left all alone. She seemed the logical person to blame my misfortune on. After all, she had left me to the wolves, so to speak, before. Hadn't she?" he said with a hint of venom in his voice.

He took another sip of tea, and then blurted, "What kind of woman abandons her child, anyway??"

Mary started to reply and then decided to hold her counsel.

"Alan looked at me for what seemed an eternity, and then said he had a story to tell me, which perhaps, if I agreed to hear him out without interruption, might just help me understand a little at to why, sometimes a desperate girl chooses to give up her most treasured possession, her baby."

Alan told David Linda's story, word for word, as he had been told by her, he then went on to explain that the girl he had just told him of was now twenty three years older, and was about to become his wife.

David congratulated him on his impending marriage. He thanked him for sharing Linda's story with him, and agreed that, yes, it did let him see the story from another's viewpoint he would never have considered. He had certainly never thought of the dilemma that his own natural mother must have had to face, and Alan had certainly given him a new insight into his plight. I realised that, for the first time in my life, I could think of my natural mother without feeling bitter." He said, a trace of a smile crossing his face.

"I remember looking at Alan Ferguson just then. He was toying with an envelope he had in his jacket pocket. He looked at me, and said that this was the most difficult decision he had ever had to make in his life, but right or wrong, he had to tell me." David heaved an emotional sigh." He then told me that he had hired a detective agency to trace Linda's child. He made it very clear that Linda knew nothing of this, it was entirely his doing, and his alone. I didn't quite understand why he was telling me this, it was after all, his own private business. Then he handed me the envelope!"

Chapter Thirteen

Linda ran to meet Marjory as soon as her eye caught sight of her in the crowd alighting from the bowels of the big airbus jet which had arrived a few minutes earlier form London. She had asked Marjory to be her bridesmaid, and her former secretary and dear friend had agreed immediately.

"You are a dark horse, Linda Cartell! You never let on for one moment that there was a man in your life! By the way, does he have a brother?" she asked before Linda had time to say anything.

"Marjory, has anyone ever told you that you have a one track mind?" Linda retorted as they went forward to the carousel to collect Marjory's luggage.

"Of course! But you can't blame a girl for trying." Marjory replied, tongue in cheek.

"Did you have a good flight up here?" Linda asked her friend as Marjory retrieved her cases from the carousel.

"Very nice, thank you. But stop holding out on me, Linda. Come on. Tell me all about your obviously wildly handsome highlander. Don't be a spoil sport!"

"You will never change, Marjory. I'll arrange a porter to take your luggage to the freight sheds to be put on our plane, and then we are going to the airport hotel for lunch, and we can have a good gossip, and I promise to tell you all about Alan'. Linda said.

"I'll take those, Linda" Dick Hays said.

"Dick. I didn't se you there. This is my friend Marjory Simons. Marjory, meet Dick Hays, our pilot." Linda said smiling broadly.

"So, you are our pilot, Dick? I have never met a pilot before. What is it like to fly a plane. I'll bet it is simply great!" Marjory said all in one breath, not giving poor Dick a chance to answer.

"If we get the chance to, in a day or so after the wedding is over, Marjory, I promise that I will take you up and let you try flying the plane for yourself." He replied, winking all the while at Linda.

"Wow! Are you kidding me or are you serious?" Marjory said, excited by the prospect of soaring into the wild blue yonder.

"I kid you not. That is a date after the wedding, if you are staying on for a few days. "Dick said.

"You are on. I do love a man of action, Linda, don't you?"

"You really are the limit Marjory. Not in the country for two minutes and you already have a date. Poor Dick doesn't know what he is letting himself in for!" Linda laughed.

"Once I get him up alone up in the clouds, he'll soon find out! Marjory quipped.

Linda told Marjory all she wanted to know about Alan over lunch, and about the highland cows that had led to their meeting, and what a fool she had made of herself! Marjory nearly fell off her chair laughing as Linda related the incident to her.

"It's all right or you to laugh, Marjory Simons. You haven't encountered the beasts yet. I hope I am there when you do!" Linda goaded with a wicked grin spread all over her face!

"Are you quite sure Alan hasn't got a brother who would is a good looking as him and also single and seeking a very good looking secretary, with a view to marriage?" Marjory queried when Linda had told her about Alan.

"You are incorrigible, Marjory. No. He has not got a brother. And, if I recall, you have just made a date with our pilot, if I'm not mistaken." Linda said, shaking her head.

"Oh yes. I forgot to ask him. What airline does he fly for, do you know?" Marjory asked.

"Didn't I tell you? Dick works for Alan. He flies Alan's aircraft."

"He what? Did you say that he flies Alan's aircraft. You mean you are marrying a man who owns his own plane? Wow! You are a lucky girl Linda. I am not jealous of course, just a very dark green with envy." Marjory replied grinning.

"You will probably turn purple in a moment when I tell you then that not only does he own his own plane, he owns three planes. One of them is a Lear Executive jet. The one we flew to Canada in." Linda said, watching her friends eyes widening as she spoke.

"That was wicked of me, Marjory. I forgot to mention that Alan is extremely wealthy. Actually, he is one of the richest men in the country. I assumed that you would figure that out pretty quickly when I told you who he really is" Linda apologised.

"You are right. I should have known that he was obviously extremely well heeled when you told me who he is. Are you positive he hasn't a brother?" Marjory joked.

They strolled along the airport concourse, pausing to look at the array of shops displaying tempting merchandise to the jet setting public. Suddenly, Marjory started to laugh heartily.

"What on earth are you laughing at, Marjory. I can't see anything funny" Linda said in puzzlement.

"I was just thinking, Linda. You were the one who always maintained that you had no time for romance! What do you have to say now, my girl?" her friend teased.

"The sad thing is that I honestly believed that when I said it, Marjory. How little I knew!" Linda replied.

"See. You should listen to Marjory. I have always said that when you have no time for romance in your life, girl, it is time to give up the ghost! By the way, where is your mum? She asked, suddenly aware that Mary Cartell wasn't there.

"She decided to have a nice relaxing day at the cottage. She thought a rest would do her the world of good before the big day tomorrow." Linda replied, innocently unaware of the drama being played out at that moment, right in the cottage!

David handed the envelope to Mary. "It is self explanatory. Please read it." He said. The envelope contained the report from the detective agency to Alan. It was a very detailed and graphic report, and Mary Cartell turned chalk white as she read.

"I just sat for a long time in silence when I read it" David said. "I simply didn't know what to say." Mary patted his hand sympathetically.

"Alan broke the silence eventually" David told her. "He said that the only thing that I had to believe was that I had already been proposed for my promotion before he was in receipt of the report. I honestly cannot bring myself to believe him!"

"David. Please take my word for this. The one thing you can and must believe, is that if Alan Ferguson said that he had not received the document before you were promoted, then that is the truth. He is a very honourable man. He would not lie to you." Mary said sincerely.

"Do, you honestly think so?" David asked, not sure whether he wanted a reply in the affirmative or the negative.

"I not only think so, David. I know so. I would stake my life on it." Mary replied positively.

Tears welled in his eyes as he suddenly spat out "It is all this Linda, what do you call her fault!"

Tears trickled down Mary's face as she rose from her chair and went through to the living room, emerging a few moments later holding a photograph in a silver frame.

"Do you remember when we met on the beach this morning. I told you that I thought I was seeing a ghost?" He nodded in reply. Mary handed him the photo, an old black and white print, many years old.

David was startled to see the image of a young man in R.A.F. uniform staring out at him. I f he hadn't known better, he would have sworn it was of him!

"The photo is of my late husband, taken when he was around your age, David. Everything that Alan told you about Linda is true. She was advised, no. ill advised by her parents. No, coerced is more honest to say, to give up her baby, and it has haunted her all of her life. David, if you must be angry with anyone, please vent your ire at the man in the photograph and at me!"

Tear streamed down her face as she spoke. "The man in the photograph you are holding is Linda's father. I am her mother, and therefore, you are my grandson!!" She broke down, sobbing uncontrollably.

David stood helpless, transfixed in utter astonishment! This complete stranger he had just poured his heart out to, was his grandmother!

Slowly, Mary's tears subsided, and at last she regained her equilibrium. She became aware of David's presence, and she reached hesitantly for his hand. He just stood in silence, staring at her. She cupped his hands very tenderly between her palms, and spoke very gently.

"David, I gave your mother very foolish advice. I have always known this, and it is the cross I have had to bear. I won't be as presumptuous as to ask for your forgiveness. I don't deserve it. But try and find it in your heart to forgive my daughter, who was a very young girl, and very ill at the time, I may add, who capitulated to her parents wishes after relentless and totally unfair pressure was inflicted upon her."

She was now squeezing his hands tightly in hers as emotion gripped her." Linda has borne an almost unbearable guilt all these years, and I have had to watch her suffer in silence, knowing that I was to blame."

Tears flowed down David's cheeks, as he faced his new found grandmother. "Please, don't distress yourself. Please." He pleaded. "I do not hate anyone, and I honestly do not blame anyone either, The past twenty four hours have been quite the most eventful of my life, and I guess I have let things get on top of me. I am very sorry for upsetting you" he said in a husky voice, and then kissed her gently on the cheek. Mary was almost overcome with emotion at that moment.

"C.C. Could you t.t.tell me where my mu.m.m..mother is?" he asked falteringly.

"Yes, of course, David. I am afraid that she has gone to Glasgow. She is meeting her bridesmaid, who is flying up from London today. I don't expect them here until around seven o'clock this evening." Mary replied, having regained her composure once again.

"I see" he replied, not too sure whether he was disappointed or relieved. "Are you going to tell her about me?" he asked Mary.

She hesitated for a moment. "Every instinct makes me want to shout it from the roof tops. But, I won't. The decision must be yours, David. And yours alone." Mary said tearfully.

"Thank you. I respect you for that. Alan said the same thing. You know, it's funny really, I didn't quite believe him when he said it would have to be my decision, and that he would honour whatever decision I made. I know now that you will both be true to your word. I also realise that Alan never told you about me either." David turned and walked smartly from the room, leaving his grandmother thrilled and bewildered, wondering if he would choose to meet his mother, or opt for the safe option and leave things as they stood.

Alan collected Linda and Marjory at the airstrip, and soon delivered them safely to the cottage. It was just after seven o'clock in the evening. After the initial greeting, Mary sat them down to a nice meal and a very welcome pot of tea for Marjory, and a pot of Colombian coffee for Linda, her favourite. "I am only spoiling you this evening, my girl. Enjoy it while you can." She wisecracked, giving Alan a wink.

"Alan, would you mind terribly if I was to come up to the house with you? I have a few details I would like to check before tomorrow." Mary said to her future son in law.

"Of course, although I am positive that everything is spot on, you know." He replied, rather curious as to why she should require to check any details at this time.

Alan and Mary left the girls eating their meal, and headed for the mansion. "What is the mystery, Mary? I know you are quite satisfied with the arrangements." He queried. Mary, a bit falteringly, related her morning to Alan.

"I am so sorry, Mary. It must have been a terrible shock for you. I never meant anything like this to happen, honestly." He said apologetically.

"Don't worry about me, Alan. I am more worried about young David. I honestly don't know what he is going to do." Mary replied.

"I am sorry I ever started this now.." Alan said regretfully. "I never imagined for a moment that it would backfire so disastrously. I took a gamble, Mary. Not out of self interest, you understand, but for Linda. I thought it would be the greatest gift I could possibly give her. I guess I handled the situation very badly."

"Don't blame yourself, Alan. I t was a very fine thing you did, most men would never dream of doing such a thing for their lover. I only regret that it would seem to have gone wrong. You have to be commended for trying, Alan. I realise that Linda may never learn of this, but I thank you on her behalf." Mary said warmly, and kissed his cheek tenderly.

"Thank you, Mary. I do appreciate that. My one true regret is that I know David would have loved Linda, and it goes without saying that she would have been the happiest woman on earth. I am sorry I failed" he said, heaving a big sigh.

David was sitting on the shore, holding a fishing rod, deep in thought, completely oblivious to the furious tugging on the line, as the fine cod he had hooked struggled for its life. He too was feeling very melancholy.

Linda sipped champagne, listening to Bret Gray, the best man, deliver the traditional best man's speech. He was very witty, a natural comedian, and everyone was laughing and happy.

The wedding ceremony had gone without a hitch, and now the festivities were really under way. Alan was looking extremely handsome indeed, dressed in full highland dress. He really suited the kilt, she thought. She made a mental note to encourage him to wear it more often. Strangely, she had noticed that both he and her mother had seemed on edge the whole day. Only natural for the bridegroom to be nervous on his wedding day and what mother of the bride isn't? Marjory had remarked when she had said to her, and she was one was one who understood such things, Linda reasoned.

The one fact that did amaze her was her own demeanour. She was as cool as a cucumber, and had been all day! Not even a single butterfly in the tummy!

The meal was simply divine, although Linda found that the courses came and went as though she were in a dream. The band struck up, and she and Alan led the first waltz, as tradition dictated.

"I do love you Alan." She whispered in his ear, as he danced her along the floor. They seemed to be floating on air.

"And I love you, my darling. I am so…." He faltered in mid entrance, and came to an abrupt halt, and stared in the direction of the door.

Linda was quite taken aback by the suddenness of his action. She was about to protest, when he just suddenly stepped aside. There in front of her stood her mother, arm in arm with a young man.

Alan squeezed her hand affectionately as she looked at David, and she knew the true happiness of a mother's love for her son!

The End